PENGUIN BOOKS

Dragons and Dynasties
—An Introduction to Chinese Mythology

Yuan Ke (b. 1916), a well-known, learned Chinese mythologist, is now a research fellow of the Academy of Social Sciences, Sichuan Province, and Chairman of the Mythology Association of China. His important works include *Dragons and Dynasties —An Introduction to Ancient Chinese Mythology, Notes to Selected Ancient Mythologies, Annotations on The Book of Mountains and Seas, Legends from Ancient Chinese Mythology* and *An Anthology of Theses on Mythology.*

He lives in Chengdu, Sichuan Province, in Southwest China.

Mythology is an important and interesting part of China's rich cultural heritage. Ideas from ancient Chinese mythology have left a strong imprint on Chinese philosophy, literature and art.

As the world tries to understand China and yet finds that China remains a myth to many, *Dragons and Dynasties* will prove most useful and appealing to both the scholar and the general reader. Written by Yuan Ke, present-day authority on Chinese mythology, translated and arranged for the Western reader by Canadian and Chinese scholars of Chinese and foreign mythology and amply illustrated, this book offers a fresh look at ancient Chinese culture.

Dragons and Dynasties

—An Introduction to Chinese Mythology

Written by Yuan Ke
Selected and translated by
Kim Echlin & Nie Zhixiong

 PENGUIN BOOKS   **FOREIGN LANGUAGES PRESS**

PENGUIN BOOKS

Published by the Penguin Group
27 Wrights Lane, London W8 5TZ, England
Penguin Books USA Inc., 375 Hudson Street, New York, New York 10014,
    USA
Penguin Books Australia Ltd, Ringwood, Victoria, Australia
Penguin Books Canada Ltd, 10 Alcorn Avenue, Toronto, Ontario, Canada
    M4V 3B2
Penguin Books (NZ) Ltd, 182–190 Wairau Road, Auckland 10, New Zealand
Penguin Books Ltd, Registered Offices: Harmondsworth, Middlesex, England

First published in the People's Republic of China by Foreign Languages
    Press, Beijing 1991–3
Published in Penguin Books 1993

CONTENTS

Introduction

Mythology is an important and interesting part of China's rich cultural heritage. Our ancestors, in their attempts to understand natural phenomena, imagined the birth of the world, and the origin of humankind and all other living things. They sang the praises of heroes who worked for the good of the common people, wished for a better life, applauded a hard-working spirit and tried to overcome and transform natural forces. Thus, Chinese mythology as we read it today gradually emerged.

The earliest Chinese mythology is believed to have begun in primitive society. The first written mythology, however, was of a much later historical period, the slave society. Despite China's long cultural history, the ancient Chinese did not have a complete anthology of mythology. Most of the myths, often in fragments, were collected in different ancient books. During the long era before China was unified in the Qin Dynasty (220–207 BC), the single book that embodied a relatively complete collection of myths was the classical work, *Book of Mountains and Seas*. Mythological fragments can be found in a great number of classical writings on history, geography, heroes and ghosts published in later times.

The myths presented in this book are all based on ancient writings, but are told vividly and in chronological order. Each is characterized by one or more of the following:

(1) Praising labour. Created by the common people, ancient mythology originated from their work. All mythological gods or deified heroes were related to labour one way or another. Often they themselves were labourers, such as Pan Gu, who separated heaven and earth; Nu Wa, who created humanity; Yi, the archer, who shot down nine of the ten scorching suns; and the Great Yu, who conquered floods. They used either magical strength or divine tactics. In some cases, they were endowed with both magical powers and resourcefulness as well as superhuman skills. In other cases, they simply transformed themselves physically to fulfil a certain task. The Great Yu, for example, turned into a

bear in order to work on the mountain cliffs to control the floods.

(2) Admiring the relentless spirit of the heroes. The myth about Gun and his son, the Great Yu, taming the floods is a typical one in this respect. Gun, who stole heavenly soil with which he tried to check the flood, was punished by a heavenly god by being pressed down under a mountain. Yet his body did not decompose even after three years. Moreover, he then gave birth to his son, Yu, who carried on his father's job of flood control. He worked for thirteen years, during which he passed his home three times, but never stopped in for a visit. His selflessness gave rise to an extremely moving story. Stories about the fairy bird, Jing Wei, who tried to fill up the sea, the Foolish Old Man who attempted to remove the mountains blocking his way, and Xing Tian whose body did not stop fighting even after his head had been cut off, all describe the firm beliefs and the unyielding spirit of the divine heroes.

(3) Glorifying the common people's resistance to dictatorial rule. One of the many stories of this nature describes how Du Bo, after being wrongly killed by King Yuan of Zhou, reappeared to take revenge. The makers of such myths showed support for the weak up against the villainous strong, the ruled up against their tyrannical rulers.

(4) Describing people's longing for love, freedom of marriage and a happy family life. Most typical is the well-known story about the herdsman and his weaver girl, who were turned into constellations and allowed to meet only once a year.

Ancient Chinese mythology, with its strong romantic touch and eternal artistic appeal, has exerted tremendous influence on the art and literature of later times, inspiring the creation of many excellent works of poetry and prose as well as acrobatic performances, songs and dances throughout Chinese history. Mao Zedong, for instance, rendered new meanings to romanticism typical of Chinese mythology in many of his poems.

This book will help readers to better appreciate Chinese classical writings, and in a broader sense, to acquire a deeper understanding of China.

Chapter 1
THE GODS OF CREATION

The First World

In the beginning the world was not differentiated from the rest of the universe; all was a mass of confusion. Then a mysterious egg appeared, containing the most ancient deity, Pan Gu. When he broke the egg, he created new life—the earth —from his own body. This story is so firmly fixed in Chinese tradition that people use the idiom "since Pan Gu created heaven and earth" to mean "since the beginning of time".

Pan Gu Opens up Heaven and Earth

Before the heavens and the earth were opened, the universe was all in darkness, a mass of confusion in the shape of a great egg. And there, in that egg, was the one called Pan Gu. He had been sleeping and growing in that egg for eighteen thousand years.

One day he opened his eyes. He looked all around and saw nothing but terrible darkness. He could hardly breathe! A rage began to grow within him. "Why am I, Pan Gu, in such darkness? Why am I in this egg?"

He flung out his arms in anger and his hand touched a big axe; no one knows where it came from. He grabbed the axe and began to swing it wildly from side to side through the mass of confusion. Then suddenly, "Crash!" the sound of a thousand thunders echoed through the universe. The great egg cracked open!

Slowly then, and quietly, all lightness rose up to form the heavens and all that was thick and heavy dropped down to form the earth.

When Pan Gu saw this, he sighed deeply, and he thought, "What if heaven and earth close up again?"

So he began to support the heavens with his head and hold

1

down the earth under his feet. When he felt the heavens and earth growing, he grew too. Each day the heavens grew one *zhang* higher, and the earth one *zhang* lower. So Pan Gu grew too each day. For eighteen thousand years he grew until the top of heaven was ninety thousand *li* away from earth. And then it was fixed. And there it stayed unchanging.

For all those eighteen thousand years Pan Gu tirelessly supported the heavens. When he saw that the heavens and earth were finally fixed, he breathed deeply one last time and wearily lay down to die. And as he was dying his body slowly began to shift, sinking and rising into the many different parts of earth.

First his breath became the winds and the clouds, and his voice turned into the thunders. His left eye became the sun and his right eye became the moon. His arms and legs and body grew up into mountain ranges. His blood spilled out into the rivers. His tendons and veins stretched into the valleys, and his muscles sank down and became rich soil. His hair turned into pearls and precious stones, and his teeth and bones became gems and metals. Even his sweat and tears fell softly as the rains and sweet dews all over the earth.

And so, from the body of Pan Gu, the world became very perfect.

The First People

After Pan Gu, the first deities on earth were thought to be the goddess Nu Wa and the god Fu Xi. The philologist Xu Shen (c. 58–147) defines Nu Wa in one of China's earliest dictionaries as being in charge of the breeding of all living things, and she tends to be popularly associated with marriage and fertility. Early stories tell how she created humanity alone, but other variants suggest that Nu Wa was both wife and sister to Fu Xi and that from their union people were created. The only surviving description of the Fu Xi story appears in a book called *Du Yi Zhi* in the Tang Dynasty (618–907), recorded by the poet Li Rong. But early murals from the Eastern Han Dynasty (25–220) in Wuliang Temple (Jiaxiang County, Shandong Province) depict Nu Wa and Fu Xi with human heads and torsos, their snakelike lower bodies intertwined, a child between them. We present three versions of the story here: the first recounts creation by Nu Wa alone; the second, based on Li Rong's account, tells of Nu Wa and Fu Xi; and the last, a version popular among southwest minority groups, shows how many mythic elements can be woven into a folktale.

Nu Wa Creates Humanity

On the earth created from the body of Pan Gu, gods began to appear. The first of them was the goddess Nu Wa, who had the head of a woman and the body of a snake and could change her shape seventy times in a single day.

When Nu Wa appeared on earth she began to walk through the quiet world, looking at everything. She was pleased by the world, but as she wandered through the stillness the silence filled her body.

She came to a spring and she squatted down to listen to the waters tumbling over the pebbles. She saw some yellow soil, and she picked up a handful and began to play, hoping to make the world a livelier place. First she wet the earth. Then she squeezed it through her fingers. Then her hands moulded a little creature like herself, and when she placed it down beside the spring it began to laugh. Nu Wa liked the noise the little creature made and so she made another and another and she placed each one upon the earth and they all laughed and danced together. They were different from the birds and animals and she called them her sons and daughters.

Nu Wa wanted to make many of these little creatures but she soon grew tired, so she reached out and took a piece of vine from the mountainside and she dipped it into her damp yellow soil. With the vine she flipped out lumps of mud as quickly as she could and they all turned into human beings. Soon she had made people everywhere.

Later Taoist stories say that this is why people are different. They say that common people were just flipped into being with a piece of rattan, but superior people were formed by the hands of Nu Wa.

One day Nu Wa was sitting listening to the laughter of all the people she had created and she thought, "When they die I will have to make more again."

She thought and thought and then she made some more men and women, and these she taught to love each other and raise children. And so it was that Nu Wa was the first matchmaker.

She invented marriage, and the people began to call her goddess of marriage and offer sacrifices to her every year. In the second month of each lunar year they celebrated Tai Lao near a temple where all the young men and women met. At this time people could marry freely under the starry sky, for all during the ceremony of Tai Lao no one would dare object to "the marriage made by the goddess".

Nu Wa's temples were built in the woods and on the streams. And after a young couple were married they returned to Nu Wa to ask for a son or a daughter.

The Marriage of Nu Wa and Fu Xi

Long ago, after the world was newly made, there lived only a sister and her brother, Nu Wa and Fu Xi, atop Mount Kunlun.

They lived there all alone since there were no other people under the heaven. In the silence of that place they wanted to create other people, but being so close to the gods, they were ashamed. And so they sought a sign.

Separately they climbed to the top of two different peaks, where they made two fires of dry grass, pine needles, and sticks. And they prayed to the heaven, saying, "If the god permits us, then the smoke of our two fires will mingle and rise into the sky. If not, the smoke will drift in different directions."

Then, looking at each other, they lit the fires and watched the smoke. Slowly, miraculously, the smoke from each fire drifted towards the other, mixing and rising, disappearing into the sky. And Nu Wa made a sweet-smelling straw fan to cover her face because she was shy, which is why brides often cover their faces. So it was that Fu Xi and Nu Wa lay together and created the first human beings.

A Southwest Creation Story

In the south people cover the roofs of their homes with thick bark. This keeps out the heavy storm rains that are so frequent and so treacherous in the summer in southern regions.

Now once a man and his two children were warm and dry inside their home during a terrible thunderstorm. The children played quietly, but as the rains drummed harder and harder the man knew that the Duke of Thunder himself must surely be near by. So with his hunting spear in one hand and an iron cage in the other, he awaited the wrath of the god. Suddenly there was a flash of lightning, and a fearsome creature stood atop a bark roof. Sparks of fire shot from his eyes and he brandished an axe through the air; his wings stretched erect and fluttered, still fresh from flight.

It was the Duke of Thunder.

Despite his terror, the brave man thrust his spear and caught the god on the waist; before the Duke of Thunder could catch his balance, the man had thrust him into the iron trap, and carried him into the house.

The Duke of Thunder huddled in a corner of the cage, and the man instructed his children, "Watch the Duke of Thunder with care. Tomorrow we will eat him for dinner."

The following morning the man prepared to go to market to buy things for his stew. He told the children, "Stay close now and guard the Duke. Whatever you do, don't give him water."

With that the man went away. After a while the Duke of Thunder, huddled in the corner against the bars, began to moan pathetically. The children did not know what was wrong with him. He groaned and opened and closed his lips drily, pleading: "I'm so thirsty, please give me a drink."

The boy refused, but as the Duke kept groaning, the girl felt sorry for him. Finally the Duke slumped into the corner, his mouth hanging open as if dead. The little girl said: "Brother, he's been in there a whole night and almost a day. I'll just give him a few drops from my brush."

And so they got the brush, dipped it in water, and let a few drops fall on the parched lips. Suddenly the Duke sprang up, and waving the children away, he burst from his cage. The children trembled, but the god only plucked a tooth from his mouth and handed it to them, saying: "Plant this in your field. If disaster happens, you may hide inside the fruit."

And, with a clap of thunder, he ascended into the sky.

Now the Duke of Thunder was known as the sender of floods, so when the father returned and heard the children's story he began to prepare. He built a strong iron ship and sent the children to plant the tooth. The tooth grew rapidly. In one day it gave a sprout, in the second a flower, and by the third day there was a great calabash lying on a vine. The children took the gourd home and opened it to find thousands of tiny teeth lining the inside. They dug them all out and found that the gourd was just big enough to crawl into.

On the evening of the third day the rains began. Winds whipped through the trees, water poured from the sky. Soon torrents rushed like wild horses over the land, covering the hills, encircling the mountains, and the fields lay under an endless sea.

The children climbed into their gourd and the man into his iron boat. As the flood waters rose higher and higher, the man sailed his boat right to the gate of heaven itself, and when he got there he pounded on the door: "Let me in! Let me in!" he called.

But the god of heaven didn't want mortals there, so he commanded the god of waters to cease the flood. And the waters fell back so violently that the man in the iron boat crashed to the ground and died. But the children in the soft gourd just bounced on the earth, and when they stopped rolling, they jumped out to have a look.

They were all alone.

The flood had destroyed everything, all people, all the fields, and they were left alone on the earth. So the brother and sister began a new life and called themselves Fu Xi, which means "gourd".

For a long time they lived quite happily, scaling the heavenly ladder, playing on heaven and earth. Then one day the brother wanted to sleep with his sister. Always she refused and ran away. One day she was running away, faster and faster around a tree, when the boy had an idea. He turned, and faced in the other direction. His sister, still running as hard as she could, ran right up against him, and so it was that they lay together.

Not long after, she gave birth to a ball of flesh. They found this creature very strange, and so they chopped it into tiny pieces and put it into a bag. They began climbing the heavenly ladder with it, but about midway a sudden gust of wind blew the bag open and scattered all those pieces of flesh into the air. Falling to earth they became men and women, and they called themselves after the places in which they landed. Those who fell on leaves were called Ye (leaf), and those who fell into the forest were called Mu (wood). And so the world had men and women once more.

The Collapse of the Heavens

After Pan Gu, Nu Wa, and Fu Xi, two other gods appeared on earth—the god of fire, Zhu Rong, and the god of water, Gong Gong. With them a new principle emerges in the stories: conflict. The earliest myths are concerned with creation, but as more gods appear, so too appear the first stories of war. These stories present an interesting contrast between creativity and destruction. Nu Wa creates people with her own hands and later takes up a light tool to mould humanity; her creation is deliberate and delicate. Gong Gong, destroyer of the earth, rams down its supports with his own head in a fit of rage—a gross, uncontrolled behaviour which hurts him too. So Nu Wa puts back the sky once more. But the original tenuous perfection of the world is lost as battles are fought on Pan Gu's body and Nu Wa, the great gentle mother, withdraws forever to the sky.

The War Between Fire and Water

There was peace for many years on this first earth when suddenly, for a reason we don't remember, the first great disaster happened—Gong Gong, god of water, decided to wage war against Zhu Rong, god of fire.

Now Gong Gong was famed everywhere for his bad temper and cruelty. He had a snake's body with a human head and bright scarlet hair. His two closest officials were no less frightening. One adviser was the powerful and wicked Xiang Liu, out of whose green, scaly body wove nine heads, each with dark, shifting eyes. The other official was Fu You. No one knows what Fu You looked like, only that when he died he turned into a terrible red bear.

Gong Gong also had a son who died on the day of the winter solstice. When he died he changed into a terrifying ghost who wandered the earth afraid of nothing but red beans. So people used to make red bean porridge every winter solstice to frighten away this ghost, son of Gong Gong.

Finally there was Gong Gong's youngest son, called Xiu. He differed from the others. He had a cheerful disposition and liked to travel from place to place by cart, foot, or ship, enjoying beautiful scenery and famous mountain look-outs. The people liked him, and when he died they named him the god of travel. Traces of him are everywhere, and when people used to give banquets for voyagers they honoured Xiu to wish the traveller safety.

No one really remembers how the battle between Gong Gong and Zhu Rong began. It is said simply that the god of water wanted to rule over the god of fire. Gong Gong led the attack on Zhu Rong from a magnificent cart drawn by two spirited dragons. His officials Fu You and Xiang Liu followed close behind, and then came all the sea nymphs and underwater creatures. They were a terrible sight, but these troops could not withstand the awful heat as they approached closer and closer to the god of fire. They began to melt and burn, and finally they scattered in all directions. So it was that the god of water, who rose from the dark fearful depths, was finally overcome by the bright, dancing god of fire.

War is never fought without loss, no matter how glorious the victory. Gong Gong's ill-natured adviser, Fu You, had leapt burning into the Huaishui River never to be seen again. Gong Gong's eldest son was probably killed at the height of the battle and, burning, he became a ghost roaming the earth and haunting people. The nine-headed monster, Xiang Liu, fled in fear and hid in Mount Kunlun, where he still may be, too ashamed to show himself to the world ever again.

But it was Gong Gong who caused the greatest disaster. Enraged as his troops scattered before the fierce flames, his hopes

of domination dashed in the fiery battle, Gong Gong ran towards Mount Buzhou, the pillar which in ancient times supported the sky. With all his power he rammed his head against the mountain, and the pillar cracked and fell in pieces, broken, cutting great rifts deep in the earth.

For a single still moment all time stopped, as if holding its breath, and finally the sky collapsed and crashed down, making chaos everywhere and leaving howling, gaping holes above. Then the world began to shift, the trees of the mountains caught fire, birds and beasts of prey screamed in terror and fled from the forest. Floods burst from cracks in the ground, submerging the plains with filthy water and creating an endless sea. And the people did not know where to go. They were threatened by constant floods and wild animals, and they lived in perpetual terror, their lives a permanent encounter with death.

But what of Gong Gong himself? He had fallen over in a faint at the impact. He lay there for some time, and when he came to, he stumbled away, not to appear again until the second disaster of the flood.

Nu Wa Mends the Sky

When Nu Wa now looked upon her children she was distressed. She sighed and decided there was nothing to do but mend the sky with her own two hands.

She gathered pebbles and rocks of many different colours from all the rivers. She built a huge fire to refine these rocks and she mixed her mortar. Then she began to fill the gaping holes in the sky, pressing and smoothing plaster into the cracks. She looked at her work and worried: "What if it falls again? I'll have to make sure it stays up!"

She went and killed a giant turtle, and she cut off his four legs and made them into heavenly pillars to prop up the four corners of the sky. So the sky became a great canopy over all the people and has never fallen down again.

During the time when the heavens collapsed, a black dragon had been terrorizing the central plain. Nu Wa decided to settle accounts. She went and killed that dragon and drove away all the scavenger birds and beasts of prey. She burnt the grasses of the plains and used the ashes to stop the flooding. Great was gentle Nu Wa, who helped her children and salvaged the world from the terrible war between fire and water.

But even though the world was mended once again, it was never the same. After Mount Buzhou was knocked over, the sky shifted northwest and the sun, the moon, and all the stars tilted, turning westward. A great depression formed in the southeast, and the waters from all the rivers and streams flowed down to create the boundless oceans.

With Nu Wa's work, slowly the earth awakened once again. Each season transformed harmoniously into the next, and the people and animals lived together peacefully. They say at that time children could play with tigers and leopards, and mothers laid their babies in sweet-smelling birds' nests. Food was so plentiful that the people left it in the fields, taking only what they needed.

Nu Wa was pleased, and she gave the people the *sheng huang*, a flute made of a half-gourd and thirteen bamboo pipes that fanned out like the tail of a bird. So they honoured Nu Wa by calling her "goddess of music". (In the southwest of China the Yao, Dong and Miao peoples still play instruments similar to this flute.)

And so, after that first great war, there was once again peace on earth.

There are many legends about what happened to Nu Wa. Some say that she died and was transformed into a thousand fairies. Other say that she rode off to the heavens in a thunder cart drawn by flying dragons. There she met the Supreme God and told him all she had done, but afterwards she retired to a life of seclusion and never again spoke of her time on earth.

Chapter   2

THE GODS DESCEND TO EARTH

The Five Emperors

Chinese mythology is derived from stories of various regions and ethnic groups. Because of this variety and their antiquity, the descriptions of the earliest gods on earth tend to vary according to the author and the historical context. In some cases we can see how several separate gods were later consolidated into a single deity. For example, some say that Fu Xi was the earliest god to appear on earth, while others say it was the sun god, Fiery Emperor. Generally the Supreme God or Yellow Emperor, who had four faces, is finally regarded as the most powerful god who came to earth; it was he who divided the earth into territories. The Yellow Emperor is thought to be the original ancestor of the Zhou nation which conquered the Yin nation in the east; thus the Yellow Emperor's stories survived and he eventually became the common ancestor of all the Han people. (Today, the Han nationality is the largest among China's fifty-six ethnic groups, making up over 93 per cent of the country's total population.) The Yellow Emperor, or Huang Di, was a part-real, part-legendary figure thought to have founded the Chinese nation around 4,000 BC. Many colourful legends about him were written down during the Warring States Period (475–221 BC). His original division of the territories provides us with a useful schematic overview of ancient China's principal gods.

After Nu Wa ascended into heaven, the gods were curious about earth and descended to see it for themselves. The God of Heaven was the Supreme Emperor on earth, and he chose yellow as his imperial colour; therefore he was also known as the Yellow Emperor. He built a magnificent palace in the centre of the world on the top of Mount Kunlun. Then he divided the earth into north, south, east and west, and assigned four important gods each a territory, a season and an imperial colour.

The east was ruled by Tai Hou, the Green Emperor, assisted by Ju Mang, the god of the forest, who held a pair of compasses. They were in charge of the spring.

14

The god of the sun, the Fiery Emperor, was in charge of the south. He is also called the Red Emperor. His assistant was his great-grandson, the god of fire, Zhu Rong. Zhu held the beam of a steelyard in his hands; together they ruled over summer.

Shao Hao, the White Emperor, was in charge of the west, assisted by Ru Shou, who always held a carpenter's square and was the god of metals. Their season was autumn.

The Black Emperor, Zhuan Xu, lived in the north. His assistant was Xuan Ming, the god of water, sometimes known as Yu Qiang, the god of the sea and the wind. Yu Qiang is pictured with the weight of a steelyard in his hands, and together these gods were in charge of winter.

The Yellow Emperor also had an assistant. He was called Hou Tu and is depicted with a piece of string in his hand. Hou Tu was also god of the underworld.

So it was that the Supreme Emperor divided the earth, and with his four faces from the top of Mount Kunlun, he could survey all the territory over which he reigned.

The Struggle for Supremacy

Certain early fragments record that the Fiery Emperor was first to descend to earth, and because of this he called the other gods together and led them in a rebellion against the Yellow Emperor. They were defeated, but the Yellow Emperor was from that time forced to assert his power until he gained final supremacy. These ancient records probably reflect a blend of myth, legend, and history regarding the early power struggles of tribal groups.

The Fiery Emperor's half-brother by the same mother was the Yellow Emperor. We don't know why these half-brothers fought. We only have records of the clash of their great primordial powers, fire and water.

The fiercest battle between the two brothers was fought at Zhuolu (in today's Hebei Province). The earth lay littered with bodies, and weapons floated on the blood, but no one was victorious.

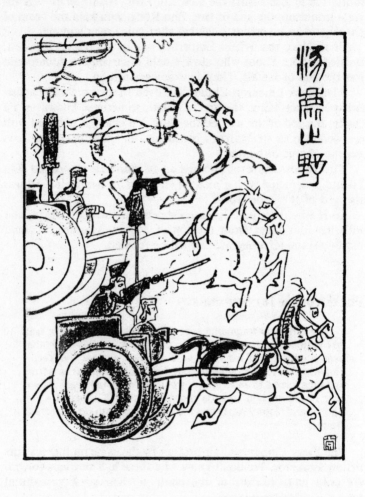

The second battle was fought on the field of Banquan. There the Yellow Emperor commanded black bears, brown bears, wolves, leopards, panthers and tigers as his troops; and birds of prey—vultures and eagles—flew above as his banners of battle. Three times they rushed into the Fiery Emperor's troops, and the third time the Yellow Emperor finally defeated his brother. So justice became the chief virtue of the people, and Huang Di, the Yellow Emperor, became absolute and supreme ruler of all heaven and earth.

The Yellow Emperor, Huang Di

In later records, after the Yellow Emperor had won the struggle for supremacy, he is said to have lived at the top of Mount Kunlun, in the centre of the world. Many stories record his acts of justice. The Yellow Emperor could punish the gods and was considered to have great power. But conflict is part of nature and so also part of the just god's rule. Following are two of many stories revealing Huang Di's pursuit of justice.

Once Gu, a god with a human face and a dragon's body (son of the god Zhu Long of Mount Zhongshan), committed a murder with another god called Qin Pi. They killed the small god Bao Jiang on the southeast side of Mount Kunlun. Immediately the Yellow Emperor sent down his officials to sentence the two murderers to death. But even in death these two gods would not rest. Gu turned into a fierce bird like an eagle whose appearance on earth always caused drought. And Qin Pi became a kind of osprey with a white head, red bill, and tiger's claws. It cried like a swan whenever it appeared, always foretelling war.

Another time a heavenly god Er Fu, who had a human face and the body of a snake, was persuaded by his evil servant Wei to kill another god, Ya Yu. Immediately the Yellow Emperor sent down his officials to arrest Er Fu. They put his left foot into a yoke, and they tied his hands and the hair of his head to an enormous tree at the top of Mount Shushu in the west, where he wasn't found until a thousand years later. As for the innocent victim, the Yellow Emperor took pity on him and ordered

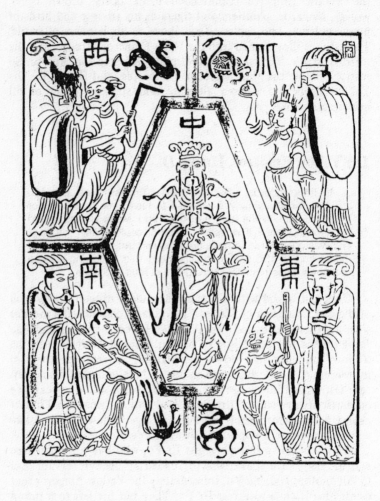

powerful witches to carry his body back to Mount Kunlun and bring him back to life. His life was indeed saved, but they could not save his original nature and he later turned into a man-eating monster who lived in a deep pool in the Ruoshui River at the foot of the mountain.

Mount Kunlun: The Earthly Home of the Yellow Emperor

Descriptions of the gods' first divine palace on earth show great concern for the physical details of immortal life— the architecture of their homes, their food and clothing, their attendants and entertainment. With the pieces of these early fragments, we can create a geographical map of the ancient imagination as it explained what happened north, south, east and west in the gods' intimate dwellings.

Mount Kunlun was the earthly home of the Yellow Emperor. The divine palace was cared for by a god called Lu Wu, who also looked after the nine heavenly cities. He was fearful-looking with a man's face, a tiger's body and nine tails.

The magnificent palace itself consisted of five cities and twelve towers. On each side were nine wells and nine gates, and the whole place was surrounded by priceless jade balustrades. The front faced east and was protected by Kaiming (facing the dawn) gate. Before this gate stood the divine Kaiming animal, who had nine heads with human faces and was the size of a tiger. It was his duty to stand guard over Mount Kunlun palace, home of a hundred gods.

Rice trees, pearl trees and jade trees grew to the west of the palace. To the east grew sand pearl and *langgan* trees. (The *langgan* were very precious, bearing fruit like pearls which was the food of phoenixes and fairy *luan* birds.) The Yellow Emperor sent the vigilant three-headed god Li Zhu to guard them, and he sat under the branches watching, letting only one head sleep at a time. The immortals themselves had very special food and drink. They drank from a clear sweet spring called Liquan near the palace, where rare flowers and aromatic grasses grew. A strange food called "eye-meat" also grew near by. It was a living thing without skeleton or

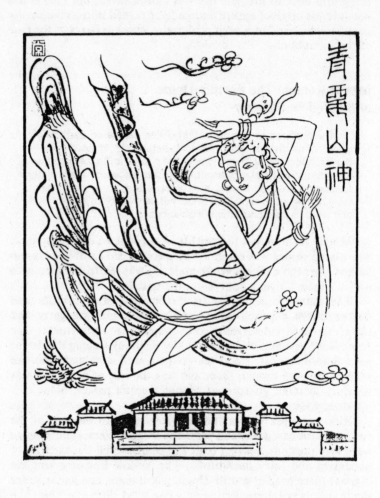

limbs, a piece of clear meat like cow's liver; pairs of eyes grew from it. Whenever the gods were hungry, they could cut off a piece and it would grow back again. Eye-meat was said to grow in many famous scenic spots and on the tombs of kings and emperors. Some said it was especially for those who inhabited the underworld. Not far from Mount Kunlun, on Mount Mishan, grew a certain soft jade from which could be squeezed soft, white jade grease. This the emperor ate each day. His leftovers were used to grow *dan* trees, which blossom only once every five years and produce fruits of five exquisite flavours. The emperor also carried some of this jade essence to the eastern part of Mount Zhongshan, where later all the gods and devils ate it, too.

If people find this jade and carve it into ornaments, it will protect them against devils and enchantment.

The divine palace was located at the peak of Mount Kunlun, which towered eleven thousand *li*, one hundred and fourteen feet, and twenty-six inches into the clouds. Nine layers of smaller mountains circled Mount Kunlun, like city walls, and at the bottom lay a deep abyss called the Ruoshui River. The palace glowed unearthly red from fire mountains flanking the other side of the abyss. These fire mountains burnt day and night steadily through strong winds and heavy rains, and in them lived mouse-like creatures, large as cows. They were covered with long, fine silky hair. They were red in the fire and when they ran out they turned snow white and water was poured on them to kill them for their hair. This was woven into cloth which did not need to be washed, but only held in fire to become clean again. All the gods used this "fire cloth" for their fine clothing.

For amusement, the Yellow Emperor would walk four hundred *li* northeast to the largest divine garden on earth at the top of Mount Huaijiang. People called this place the Hanging Garden. From there led the road to the heavens. Ying Zhao, a god with a human face, striped horse's body, and wings on his back, took care of these gardens. He was known for his sharp cries as he flew over the earth.

From the Hanging Garden, the Supreme Emperor could look back to his red-glowing palace on Mount Kunlun. To the west he could see the great lake Jize reflecting the clouds in the sky. Emerald trees grew on the shores of this lake, where the first

ancestor of the Zhou nation, Hou Ji, lived. To the north was Mount Zhupi, where eagles and vultures soared. In this great mountain lived the famous ghosts Huai Gui and Li Lun. And the lofty Mount Hengshan rose in the east, home of the You Qiong ghosts. Below the Hanging Garden the Yaoshui spring bubbled into Yaochi Lake near Mount Kunlun. The clear spring was guarded by a fierce eight-legged ox-like god with two heads and a horse's tail. This god's voice was like a horn, and wherever he went there was war. The palace was a wondrous place of rare animals and gardens, where gods wandered among precious jade and jewels tasting pleasures almost as exquisite as those they could find in the heavens.

Such then is what the fragments tell us about Mount Kunlun, home of the first gods who came to live on earth.

The Yellow Emperor Loses His Precious Pearl

The Yellow Emperor often liked to travel between the heavens and his divine earthly palace. Once when he was travelling along the Chishui River, he lost his wonderful shining black pearl. He called for his most intelligent god, Zhi, to go and look for it, but after long searching the god came back empty-handed. Then the Yellow Emperor called for Li Zhu, the god who looked after the palace's precious trees. Li Zhu had three heads and six eyes which radiated light, but he too searched for the lost pearl in vain. Then Chi Gou, god of eloquence, was summoned, but eloquence is no remedy for a lost pearl, and he also failed.

Finally the only one who hadn't searched was Xiang Wang, the most careless god in the divine world. Xiang Wang received the Yellow Emperor's order and indifferently sauntered along the Chishui River, glancing casually about as he went. And, suddenly, of all things he noticed something shining in the tall grass —the black pearl!

The Yellow Emperor had given it up for lost, and he was amazed that careless Xiang Wang had found it. Convinced that he had judged the god wrongly, he left it with Xiang Wang for safekeeping.

There is a Chinese saying: "It is easy to change rivers and

mountains, but hard to change a person's nature." Xiang Wang casually slipped the shining pearl in his sleeve and continued meandering along. Now, the mischievous daughter of Zhen Meng heard the whole story and stole the pearl away. Xiang Wang reported the theft, and the Yellow Emperor, regretting his misplaced trust, sent some officials to look into the matter. The daughter of Zhen Meng, fearing punishment, swallowed the precious pearl and jumped into the Wenchuan River (now the Minjiang River in Sichuan Province). She swam a great distance and turned into a spirit with a horse's head and a dragon's body named Qi Xiang. She became the water spirit who helped Yu regulate the Wenchuan River after the great flood.

Some legends say the black pearl was never found. But others say it stayed on the bank of the Chishui River, where it took root and grew into a magnificent tree that looked like a cypress; this tree twisted strangely so that the local people called it the "three-trunked tree", and it bore bright pearls on every leaf.

God of the East: Tai Hou

The ancient Chinese empires tended to expand eastward from the basin of the Yangtze River. Thus the eastern gods were constantly threatened by the gods of the invaders, and nowhere is this better illustrated than in the story of the god of the east himself. Tai Hou was the god of the Zhou nation. Among the Yin people, the god of the east was called Di Jun or Di Ku. Because the Yin people were conquered by the Zhou, naturally the Zhou god, Tai Hou, emerged as supreme. We will present his stories here, and the stories of the others at the beginning of Chapter 4.

Strange Birth

It is said that in a place dozens of million *li* northwest from China there was a utopian state called Huaxushi, which was too far away for any of the ancient people to reach. In that state there were no warriors of any kind. People moved underwater without drowning and walked through fire without burning. They walked through the air as if it were earth; clouds could not impair their sight nor thunder their hearing. Their lives were wholly harmonious with nature, and some say they were even half-immortals.

A girl named Hua Xu lived there. One day she was walking by a place called Leize, which means "marshland of the thunders", when she saw an enormous footprint. She was curious and placed her own tiny foot into it. As she did so, a strange quiver passed through her body. Thus she became pregnant and, soon after, she gave birth to a son called Tai Hou. (We don't know whose footprint it was; but the god of thunder, with a human head and dragon's body, lived in that marsh. Tai Hou had a man's face but he may have had a snakelike body, so perhaps they shared one blood.)

Powers and Gifts

In ancient times there were two kinds of heavenly ladder: one from the mountains and one from the trees. The heavenly ladder to Mount Kunlun was dangerous and difficult to climb because of Kunlun's surrounding fire mountains and the treacherous abyss of the Ruoshui River. But in the wilderness at Dukuang in the southwest was a heavenly ladder coming from a tree called *Jianmu*. *Jianmu*'s tall branches reached into the clouds, and the top branches circled and entwined in the shape of an umbrella. The *Jianmu* heavenly ladder was thought to have been in the centre of the world, and it was here that the gods climbed between heavens and earth.

Now Tai Hou too had the power to climb the heavenly ladder, and because of this he was made god of the east, assisted by Ju Mang, the god of the forest. Ju Mang was the son of Shao Hao, god of the west; he had a human face and the body of a bird, and he rode two dragons and held a pair of compasses which symbolized spring and life.

Tai Hou was loved for the things he gave humanity. There are many stories about the gift of fire: some say the Suiren people made it first; others say it was given by the Yellow Emperor; but many acknowledge Tai Hou as the giver of this great gift. Tai Hou is also called Pao Xi, which means "meat that is not raw".

Tai Hou invented the *se*, an instrument with twenty-four strings for which he composed a piece of music called "Jia Bian". His daughter was Mi Fei, who became the fairy of the Luoshui River, where she drowned. She later married He Bo, god of the rivers.

Tai Hou also taught the people how to make fishing nets and how to fish, and one of his officials, Mang Shi, whose other name might be Ju Mang, adapted this net for bird-hunting.

But perhaps Tai Hou's greatest gift was the power to contemplate the future. Tai Hou created a series of eight diagrams based on the symbols of everything in the world. He made ☰ heaven; ☷ earth; ☵ water; ☲ fire; ☶ mountain; ☳ thunder; ☴ wind; ☱ marsh. Then he taught the people how to read these signs. Tai Hou was born in the place of no barriers, and he taught people to contemplate time, the greatest barrier of all. This was Tai Hou's gift of divination.

God of the South: The Fiery Emperor

The Fiery Emperor served as god of the south. His various other names were Red Emperor, God of the Sun, and Divine Peasant. With his assistant and great-grandson, Zhu Rong, the Fiery Emperor ruled over twelve thousand *li* in the south. He was a great favourite with the people and was said to have given them grain and medicine.

The First Grain

The Fiery Emperor, half-brother of the Yellow Emperor and God of the Sun, had the head of an ox and the body of a human being.

When he first appeared on earth, he found so many people that the fruit trees were already barren and people were beginning to eat animal meat. So he taught them how to plant the five cereals, making the sun give enough light to grow them abundantly. Because the people were grateful to the Fiery Emperor for this, they called him Divine Peasant.

Some say that the first grains fell from the heavens, and the
Fiery Emperor taught people how to cultivate the soil and sow
the seeds. Others say that a red bird flew overhead carrying
nine seedlings. As the bird passed, the grains fell and the Fiery
Emperor began cultivation. At this time, too, he showed people
how to make market-places and keep time according to the sun.
In this way, people learned to trade and barter for what they
needed.

Not only was the Fiery Emperor the god of agriculture, he
was also the god of medicine. He gave plants their healing
properties by lashing them with his divine whip. Some he made
poisonous, some not; some became cool, some hot. The Divine
Peasant made many plants to be used by the people against
disease.

Some accounts say that the Divine Peasant was poisoned
seventy times in a single day while testing all the plants. Some
say he even died of it. His cauldron for boiling herbs is still in the
Shenfu Mountains in Taiyuan County, Shanxi Province. And in
the Chengyang Mountains we can still see the places where he
whipped the herbs.

The Three Daughters of the Fiery Emperor

The Fiery Emperor had many children, but it is his three
daughters who are best known to the Chinese people. They had
three different natures and three different fates. These daughters probably came from the marriage of the Fiery Emperor
and a mortal woman.

The nameless daughter was the most ambitious; she loved
people, but she was tempted by the life of the immortals. One
day she learned that one of her father's mortal officials had
become a fairy, and immediately she went to him and told him
she wanted to be a fairy, too.

This official was called Chi Songzi, and he was in charge of
the rains in the south. He was said to eat clear jade, a magic
stone now called crystal. He took this to purify himself, and he
had also learned the power of burning in the white centre of a
flame, floating up and down with the fire. Finally he became

a fairy and went to live in Mount Kunlun, where he floats in the clouds over the summit whenever it is going to rain. The Fiery Emperor's eldest daughter watched, and soon she too turned into a fairy and went away to the mountains with Chi Songzi.

Another daughter was called Yao Ji, and she was light-hearted and cheerful. She died very young, before she was even married, and was buried with great sorrow on the east side of Mount Wushan. But this gentle creature did not want to go to the underworld, and so she became a tree. Each spring this tree blossoms bright with yellow flowers, and each autumn it pro-duces sweet fruit—whoever eats this fruit will become very beautiful.

After many seasons, the God of the Heaven took pity on young Yao Ji and allowed her to be the goddess governing the clouds and rains of Mount Wushan. Each morning her gentle beauty is seen in the colourful mist rising over the peaks. Only at the melancholy twilight time do her tears drop as misty rains over the trees and mountain valleys.

Perhaps the most poignant tale is that of Nu Wa, the Emperor's third daughter. Like her sisters, young Nu Wa had a happy disposition. One day she took a small skiff to row upon the East Sea, for she loved to watch the sunlight sparkle on the waves. She rowed farther and farther away from home, and when one of those sudden ocean storms blew up, her light boat overturned and she fell overboard into the rough waters. The poor girl drowned in grief and anger at having to leave so soon the world she loved. She turned into a *jingwei* bird, which looks like a crow with a shining head, white bill and red claws.

She vowed to fill up the sea which had stolen her life. Each day the brave little bird flew back and forth carrying twigs and pebbles, dropping them into the East Sea. And the waves laughed, "Aiee! Foolish bird! Never in a hundred thousand years will you be able to fill up the sea. Go play somewhere else."

But the little one just flapped with more determination, calling out over the laughter of the waves, "I will never stop, not even in a hundred million years. I will continue to fill you until the end of the world."

Later she found a seagull mate, and all their girl-children looked like *jingwei* herself, and the boys looked like their father, the seagull. Today they still fly around the place in the East Sea where Nu Wa drowned. Her determination inspired the people, and the Chinese still say "*Jingwei* fills up the sea" to describe someone with an indomitable spirit.

Local people also call *jingwei* "Innocent Bird", "Promised Bird" and "Ambitious Bird". Some call her "Bird of the Emperor's Daughter", and in this way her spirit has entered the hearts and minds of the Chinese people.

God of the West: Shao Hao

Shao Hao had strange and wonderful parents. His beautiful mother was a weaver in the Palace of Heaven. After weaving late into the night she liked to row a raft along the Silver River (Milky Way) to an old mulberry tree called Qiongsang. The Qiongsang tree was more than a thousand *zhang* high, with leaves red as the autumn maple. This tree bore fruit only once every ten thousand years, and whoever ate it would live as long as heaven and earth.

Now at that time there was a very handsome young man who called himself Prince of the White Emperor. He too often came to the Silver River from the sky because he was the Morning Star. He saw the maiden resting under the old mulberry tree, and he played his stringed *se* for her and sang. They fell in love and one night they forgot to return to their homes. The prince leapt on to the maiden's raft and together they floated down to the sea. A branch of laurel was their mast, a stalk of sweet grass their flag. From a precious piece of white jade they carved a turtledove which they placed atop the mast to tell the wind direction in every season. And ever since, sailors have made engravings of this "knowledge of the winds" bird to hang on their boats and their homes.

So the lovers, Morning Star and the maiden, floated shoulder to shoulder on the raft, playing the *se*, singing songs to one another. Their immortal music echoed along the Silver River, and from this joyful love was born a son who would one day govern the western realms: his name was Shao Hao.

God of the North: Zhuan Xu

Zhuan Xu was the great-grandson of the Yellow Emperor and appeared at about the same time as the god of the west. It is said that the Yellow Emperor and his wife had a son called Chang Yi who committed a crime in the heavens and was banished to Ruoshui (in today's Sichuan Province). Chang Yi had a son called Han Liu who was very foolish-looking with a long neck, small ears, a human face, and a pig's mouth. He had pig's feet under which rolled dazzling wheels of fire. He married a woman called Ah Nu (daughter of Nao Zi Shi), who bore Zhuan Xu, god of the north.

The Heavenly Ladder Destroyed

At first Zhuan Xu had helped his uncle, god of the west, Shao Hao, to govern the kingdom of birds so that by the time he returned to the north he was capable of ruling the twelve thousand *li* of the north with his uncle and faithful assistant Yu Qiang.

Now at this time the Yellow Emperor had been waging battle for several years with the Miao people led by Chi You. Being tired of the duties of power, he was looking for a successor and chose his great-grandson Zhuan Xu to ascend the divine throne.

They say there is order at the core of the greatest disorder. When Zhuan Xu came to the throne, he looked into the turmoil around him to provide a way to peace. The god Chi You had brought much suffering to earth, and Zhuan Xu derived this conclusion: "There are more disadvantages than benefits when mortals and immortals live together. And so they must be separated."

In those days there was still a ladder between heaven and earth. The gods and fairies and witches all came and went easily between the two places. Sometimes when people were in great trouble they too could struggle up to the heavenly palace to ask for help. And so in those early times the difference between gods and mortals was not so very great.

But Zhuan Xu changed all that.

He realized that Chi You had descended to the south secretly to instigate the Miao people to rebellion. He forced them to fight with cruel instruments of torture, and had been reported to the Yellow Emperor by the innocent ghosts he had killed.

Zhuan Xu reviewed all these events and feared that uprisings might recur, and so he ordered two gods, Chong and Li, to cut off the way between heaven and earth. Immortals could no longer easily descend to earth; mortals could no longer ascend to heaven. They lost their freedom. But the world became more orderly. The god Chong was then assigned to the heavens, and Li assigned to earth. Li's son, Yi, had a human face and no arms. His feet grew out of his head, and they were used to form a heavenly gate in the west behind which all the suns and moons and stars set each night. So it was that Yi helped his father in the new order after Chong and Li cut off the old way between heaven and earth.

Zhuan Xu's Children

The records frequently tell of Zhuan Xu's zealous discipline. One story recounts how he forbade women to stand in the way if they met a man approaching on the same path. It is said that if a woman remained in the path, witches would display her in a public place.

In another tale Zhuan Xu punished a sister and a brother who lived together as husband and wife. Enraged at their incest, he cast them into a forest deep in a mountain, where they died of hunger and cold still embraced in one another's arms. A divine bird flew over and saw them and pitying these poor lovers covered their bodies with immortal grass. Seven years passed, and they came to life again, their bodies linked and transformed into a strange man with two heads, four hands and four feet. The offspring of these two became a tribe called Mengshuang.

Zhuan Xu had three wicked sons who all died very young. One became the ghost of malaria; he lived in Jiangshui, spreading this dreaded disease of chills and fevers wherever he could. The second lived in Ruoshui. He was a demon who looked like a three-year-old boy but with red eyes, long ears, black hair and a black translucent body through which you could see red veins. He would attract people by crying like a child. And the last boy transformed himself into a demon who hid in the corners of houses, frightening children, making them sick, and giving them skin ulcers. These three sons were so threatening that on the eighth day of the first lunar month people held ceremonies to drive them away.

Zhuan Xu had another son called Tao Wu or Nan Xun, which means "fierce and untamed". It is said that he was brutal and larger than a tiger with hair two feet long all over his body. He had a human face, a pig's mouth and the tail and claws of a tiger. He lived alone on the wild plains, and no one dared come near him.

The Secret of Longevity

The most renowned descendant of Zhuan Xu was his great-grandson Peng Zu, whose birth was very strange. It is said that a man named Lu Zhong married Nu Gui, the daughter of Gui Fang Shi. Now Nu Gui was pregnant for three years but could not give birth. Finally her left armpit was opened and three children came out; then from her right armpit, three more children were taken, of which the last was Peng Zu. At the end of the Yin Dynasty, Peng Zu was already seven hundred and sixty-seven years old. The King of Yin sent for Peng Zu and asked the secret of his longevity, but Peng Zu made only this answer:

"Of course there are ways of lengthening life, but I know nothing of them. My own father died before I was born, and my mother when I was only three years old. I was sickly as a child and in my first hundred years I lived through the upheavals caused by the Quanrongs, so I moved to the Western Regions. Since my youth I have had forty-nine wives, and my fifty-four children have all died young. My life has been hard, my experience has made me weary. Look how thin I am. I am afraid I will die young. How can I, of all people, tell you the secret of longevity?"

And so he made a sign and disappeared. It is said that seventy years later people saw him moving slowly on the back of a camel across the horizons on the western border of Liusha State.

Many have tried to guess how he lived to be more than eight hundred years old. Some say he took a cassia herb. Others say he practised special breathing. But these things are probably not true. The real reason is that Peng Zu was an excellent cook of a wild chicken dish which he once offered to the God of Heaven.

The Death of Zhuan Xu

It is said that the gods who lived on earth could die just as mortals did. But strange signs sometimes appeared.

When Zhuan Xu died, a strong wind blew from the north and the water of underground springs burst out from under the earth. A snake turned into a fish, and some say that Zhuan Xu himself turned into a strange kind of half-man, half-fish creature called the *yu fu*, or the Fish Man.

God of the Underworld: Hou Tu

The most trusted assistant of the Yellow Emperor was Hou Tu, who helped in the upper world but was primarily god of the underworld. He is usually depicted with a piece of string in his hand and had enormous power, for bad spirits and ghosts haunted those early peoples and they looked to Hou Tu for protection. But Hou Tu did not rule alone. Other gods were needed to help him.

First there were the sixteen "gods who patrol the darkness". These sixteen roamed the wild southern plains at night. They had small faces and red shoulders growing straight from their arms; their duty was to patrol against ghosts who wanted to disturb the sleep of the Yellow Emperor.

People say that Hou Tu did not rule directly over the ghosts of the underworld himself; this task belonged to two brothers, Sheng Tu and Yu Lei. The gate to the underworld was at Taodu Mountain in the East Sea. A golden rooster stood there on top of an enormous peach tree which spread its shade three thousand *li* in all directions from the top of the mountain. With the first grey streaks of dawn, the golden rooster crowed after the jade rooster in Fusang, and the brothers Sheng Tu and Yu Lei ascended the gate of the underworld to survey all the ghosts who wandered at night but had to return at dawn. Any ghosts who harmed earth's people were tied up with a rope of reed and thrown down the mountain to a huge tiger who swallowed them whole.

This story has been known for centuries by the Chinese people. They used to carve statues of the two brothers from the wood of the peach tree and, on the eve of Spring Festival, hang them on their doors. Some people drew pictures of the gods with their names inscribed below to paste on the portals of the doors; then they drew tigers on the door. All these images were to frighten away the ghosts and spirits and were replaced each year. The famous poem "Spring Festival" by Wang Anshi, a Song Dynasty poet, recalls the custom:

> *Crack of fireworks, old year passes,*
> *New spring breezes warm Sutu wine.*
> *A thousand doors welcome the morning sun,*
> *New peach carvings replace the old.*

Demons, Giants and Ghosts: The Other Realms of Heaven and Earth

Besides the Yellow Emperor on Mount Kunlun and the gods of the four directions, there were many other lesser gods living in the heavens as well as in earthly rivers, oceans and mountains. Giants, dwarfs and other sometimes partly human beings lived in distant states.

The Yellow Emperor's Procession

Once the Yellow Emperor was walking on Mount Hengshan to the east of Mount Kunlun. There he happened to meet a divine talking animal called Bai Ze. Bai Ze knew everything about spirits and demons. He knew about those living in forests and pools of water, about those in the mountains and in the rivers and on the roadsides. Hearing all that Bai Ze described, the Yellow Emperor was humiliated that he, highest emperor in heaven and earth, didn't know these things. And so he asked Bai Ze to draw all the spirits and make notes. So Bai Ze did, and he drew twelve thousand five hundred and twenty different demons, goblins, ogres and spirits.

Then the Yellow Emperor called all these gods and spirits together at the Xitai Mountains. In a magnificent procession he sat on a great chariot drawn by an elephant, with six flying dragons behind him. The *bifang* bird, which looks like a crane but has a human face, white mouth, green and red striped body, and only one leg, sat in the carriage with him. (This bird was said to cry out the sound of its own name and create strange fire wherever it wanted.) Before the elephant-drawn carriage Chi You led his jackals, wolves and tigers to make the way. A god of wind and a god of rain cleaned the road for the procession. Fei Lian was the name of the wind god, and he had a horned bird's head, though his body was a deer's with leopard spots and a snake's tail. The rain god was called Ping Hao or Ping Yi. He looked like a silkworm and he could turn a clear sky into a heavy storm in seconds.

Following the wagon were all the strange ghosts and demons, and flying above were phoenixes and huge winged snakes. The Emperor was so pleased with the magnificence of his following that he burst into divine music, powerful and heart-thrilling, called "Qingjiao". This music could shake all the heavens and earth, touching gods and ghosts alike.

Giants

On the Bogu Mountains near the Dayan Mountains in the East Sea, where the sun and the moon rise, lived giant people. At the top of Bogu was a clearing called "Place of Giant People". Their smallest rowboats were bigger than battle ships; their pregnancies lasted thirty-six years, and when they arrived in the world they were already enormous with white hair. They could fly with the clouds before they learned to walk, for it was true that they were the descendants of dragons.

Giants also lived in the divine realms, in the heavens and the underworld. Guarding the gate of the divine world was an enormous nine-headed monster who could pull up a handful of trees like dry autumn grass. The gates of the underworld were protected by the giant Tu Bo, who had a pair of long, sharp horns and an enormous belly. He battled his insatiable hunger by chasing the black ghosts of the darkened realms and catching them with his bloody paws.

Dwarfs and Little People

Little people were thought to live only on the earth. In the state of Jiaoyao near the South Sea lived a group of very intelligent little dwarfs, the tallest of which measured a slight three feet while many were only a few inches high. They wore clothes like ours, lived in tidy little caves, and could construct many clever inventions. One record tells how they presented to King Yao arrows which needed no plumes to fly. They cultivated the fields and feared only the white crane who ate them. It is said that their neighbours in Daqin State who were ten *zhang* tall often came to help them.

There were some little people called Jingren or Junren who lived for only one day. They lived in the Yinshan Mountains where there grew a kind of tree called Nushu (female tree), which produced tiny naked babies each morning when the sunlight first touched the earth. As the sun rose, the babies jumped down from the trees and ran about playing all day until sunset, when they vanished. The next day the trees produced another crop of babies.

In the West Sea, in a kingdom called Dashi, were magic trees with green branches and red leaves which each day produced little men only six inches long. Their heads were connected to the branches, and when people walked by they smiled and waved their hands and legs. Junren means "mushroom people", and it was said that if they were picked from the tree they died immediately, and if eaten they could make the eater immortal.

The fullest account of little people is a fable in the classic *Zhuang Zi*. Now, according to the tale, there were once two kingdoms called Chushi and Manshi. Chushi was located on the left antenna of a snail and Manshi on the right. The kings of these two territories warred against each other fiercely, always trying to gain territory. Their fighting was bitter indeed, and when war broke out, thousands of soldiers soon lay dead on the battle ground. The stronger army was relentless until their victory was complete.

Another record mentions the state of Hu in the West Sea where there were men and women only seven inches tall. These little people were known for their politeness, for bowing to each other with clasped hands. They lived to be three hundred years old and could travel a thousand *li* in a day. The only thing they feared were sea swans which would eat them, but the little people could live inside the bellies of these birds and so they too could fly a thousand *li* in a day.

A last group of little people known for their politeness were those who lived in the state of Junzi, which means "gentle people". These little people were said to dress very well and to wear a double-edged sword hanging from their belts. Each person kept two tigers as servants, but all would bow courteously to each other in the road so that conflicts never arose. Besides ordinary food they ate a special flower called *mujin* (rose of Sharon) which grew throughout the state. The *mujin* is a lovely, delicate flower that blooms in the morning and withers in the evening. The Junzi people would steam the withered flowers to eat, and these short-lived flowers were thought to give the little people long life.

Chapter 3
WARS OF THE GODS

The First Uprising

The stories of the Yellow Emperor (which predate the Shang Dynasty) mirror a world in which the struggle for territorial power was continuous. From the four directions, north, south, east and west, the gods vied for more than their allotted twelve thousand *li* and struggled against other gods coming from the heavens who also wanted a share of the earth. Most of the fragments which survive about the Yellow Emperor recount these battles. In one of the earliest tales, the four great gods, the Green Emperor of the east, the Red Emperor of the south, the White Emperor of the west, and the Black Emperor of the north, all plotted together against the Yellow Emperor. But as ruler he reasoned thus:

"If rulers make trouble against the emperor, then their people will feel troubled and uneasy. If a ruler loses his country, his officials must become the officials of another and their loyalties are never certain. Unease will prevail throughout the land. After all, bandits are not kept to become perils to the people, and so I, Supreme Emperor of all gods and people, will not allow these bandits from the four directions to plot against me. How can I bear such offence to the harmony of my subjects?"

And with that he led his armies against each emperor in turn until all were conquered.

Chi You Challenges the Yellow Emperor

Some people think that Chi You was a ferocious god in the heaven, but others say that Chi You is the name of a brave tribe of giants from the south who were descendants of the Fiery Emperor. The tribe was supposed to be made up of Chi You's eighty-one brothers (some records say seventy-two), all huge, powerful and valiant. There are many contradictory descriptions of this tribe. Some say they had bronze heads and

41

foreheads, that their bodies were animal but that they spoke human language. Others say that the Chi You had human bodies, cow's feet, six hands and four sharp eyes. Some count eight hands and eight feet; others say that they had a sharp horn on their heads. Most consistent with their claimed lineage from the Fiery Emperor is that they looked like him with a human body and the head of an ox. But the stories around these southern giants vary. Chi You ate all kinds of food: sand, stone, lumps of iron. They liked to make war arms: lances, spears, axes, shields, bows and arrows.

Once the god Chi You was invited to the Yellow Emperor's grand assembly of the gods and demons of heaven and earth, and when he surveyed the assembly he arrogantly judged them to be puffed up with weak ostentation. He believed that if he were ever able to engage the Emperor in battle he would certainly win.

With that initial fanning of his ambitions he decided to build his reputation by seizing the throne of his forefather, the Fiery Emperor, before taking on the Supreme Emperor. Chi You, with his brutal troops of demons and devils, led a surprise attack on the peaceful old Divine Peasant and his assistant Zhu Rong, god of fire. These two leaders did not favour subjecting their people to the sufferings of war, and so they escaped south to Zhuolu and allowed Chi You to take over the throne. With the pride of arrogance, Chi You bestowed upon himself the title of Fiery Emperor as if he were a direct successor to the old god. Ambition had driven him to seize the throne, and ambition would now turn his avarice to the throne of the Yellow Emperor himself.

Needing more troops, he forced the brave Miao people, descendants of the Yellow Emperor, to join him and expand his forces. Then he led the Miao and all his iron-headed brothers to the famous ancient battlefield of Zhuolu, where the original historical war had been fought between the Yellow Emperor and the former Fiery Emperor leading the gods of the four directions.

We remember that the former Fiery Emperor had only recently escaped to Zhuolu. The Yellow Emperor guessed Chi You's strategy when he began to march and now grew angry.

At first he sent messengers to try to dissuade those oxen-headed troops from their pursuit of power. But arrogant Chi You ignored him.

And so erupted the great war.

Chi You led the fearless Miao, his brothers, and demons and devils. The Yellow Emperor led gods and ghosts, black bears, brown bears, leopards, jackals and tigers. The two armies were well-matched.

These wars were full of tricks and subtle manoeuvres. One time Chi You covered the whole battlefield with thick, white fog until the Yellow Emperor's troops could see nothing at all. The horned oxen troops appeared and disappeared in the fog, slashing, slicing, stabbing into thin air. Unearthly shrieks and groans of battle filled the fog; tigers, bears and wolves panicked and rushed in every direction.

Finally the Yellow Emperor on his chariot raised his precious sword and cried out: "Escape, run out of this fiendish cloud!"

"Escape! Escape!" echoed lost voices.

However, the gods and ghosts were as helpless as the Emperor himself; they felt themselves wrapped not in ordinary cloud but in a great piece of white gauze. Suddenly the Yellow Emperor noticed that a little god reputed for his intelligence, Feng Hou, was sitting in the chariot falling asleep. The Yellow Emperor lashed out angrily: "You there! We are in great danger and you can think only of sleeping!"

"Impossible to sleep at the moment, my lord," answered the bright-eyed little god, "I was just thinking."

True enough, the old immortal had indeed been thinking. And in his mind had appeared the form of the Plough (Big Dipper constellation). The Plough points always in the same direction, and he thought to himself, "If I could design something like that, we could tell what direction we were headed no matter where we were attacked."

He meditated on his scheme, gathering together all his intelligence and magic powers. Suddenly the idea of a South-pointing Chariot appeared before him. At the front of the chariot stood a small iron man, his hand stretching out in front; he was connected to a gear mechanism that enabled his finger to point south no matter which way the cart turned. The Yellow Emperor's troops quickly constructed the device, and riding in the South-pointing Chariot, the Yellow Emperor finally led his army out of the terrible cloud.

Having suffered the humiliation of being lost in clouds, the Yellow Emperor hated Chi You and began to plan his revenge. He himself had a divine winged dragon called Ying Long who used to live on Mount Xiongli at the distant border of the south. The dragon was a water-gatherer and could cause heavy rains, so the Yellow Emperor commanded him to the battlefields.

But Chi You knew that his enemy would not suffer his defeat quietly, so he had quickly sought out reinforcements from his old friends the Master of Wind and the Master of Rain. Even before the Ying Long dragon had finished preparing for battle, those two began to cast down their powers, blowing strong winds and beating heavy rains upon him. So it was that Ying Long was thwarted before the battle even began and the Yellow Emperor's troops once more lay close to defeat.

From a nearby hill, the Yellow Emperor had been surveying the entire battle. Seeing that his winged dragon was no match for Chi You's men, he resorted to his alternative strategy and sent his daughter Ba into the fray.

Now Ba usually lived on Gonggong Terrace on Mount Xikun, and although she was not beautiful, clad always in green and bald-headed, she had the power to store a great deal of heat in her body. She walked calmly to the battlefield and allowed her tremendous heat to radiate outwards into the winds and rains. At once they were forced to flee and the sun began to shine brightly over the battlefield. Having fallen back in astonishment, Chi You's brothers were for a moment distracted and vulnerable, and Ying Long seized his moment of advantage. He charged forward. He scattered the troops and killed a large number of the Miao rebels and even a few of the iron-headed brothers.

Despite those temporary losses, Chi You and his brothers had the power to fly—in the sky and all along the steep slopes of the protective mountains. Indeed, they had fled for the moment. But the Yellow Emperor knew his opponent. He was deeply troubled, for he knew that the powerful Chi You and his apparently indomitable troops would not give up. As the war dragged on, his own peace-loving troops were losing morale. Day and night did the Yellow Emperor trouble over these things.

At length, he worked out a new strategy which would depend on the high spirits of the army. He needed to create something that would fill the hearts of his men with heady victory. And so he invented the drum.

He chose for the skin of his new drum the *kui*, which was an underwater beast from Liubo Mountain in the East Sea. It was grey and looked like an ox without horns. Although it had only one leg, it sometimes rushed out of the sea leaving violent storms in its wake. It would open its mouth to roar like thunder, and its body shone like the sun and the moon.

The Yellow Emperor sent some of his best men to the East Sea to capture the creature. They did, and skinned it and dried the hide in the sun for the top of the drum.

For drumsticks the Yellow Emperor sought out Lei Shen, or Lei Shou, a strange creature with a human head and a dragon's body. He was a god of thunder; in fact, some say Fu Xi had been born when his mother stepped into Lei Shen's footprint. To amuse himself Lei Shen used to tap on his round belly to hear the rolling thunders that echoed from him. The Yellow Emperor wanted him. And so, according to his command, Lei Shen was killed and his two largest bones brought to the Supreme Ruler.

Now they were ready to inaugurate the drum. Lifting the enormous drumsticks, the Yellow Emperor struck the *kui* hide stretched tight over the barrel. A sound, as from no drum ever before or since, rolled from the instrument, louder than the thunders themselves, echoing five hundred *li* away.

Leading his troops once again, the Yellow Emperor went to challenge Chi You's men. As soon as the two armies were face to face, the Yellow Emperor struck the drum nine times. Suddenly the mountains trembled and the valleys quaked. Even the sky changed colour. The divine troops rushed forward while Chi You's army was paralysed by the sound.

That battle was the biggest victory the Yellow Emperor ever won. Many of Chi You's brothers were killed and the Miao people suffered heavy casualties. Half of the rebel troops were killed in that famous battle of the drum. But valiantly the rebel Chi You gathered together his disbanded soldiers and stragglers; and sent some of his men to seek help from the giants in the north.

A Tale of Chi You's Giant Troops: Kua Fu Tries to Catch the Sun

In the north, under the reign of Hou Tu, was the underworld which was called Youdu or "dark city". Here all things were black: black snakes, black leopards, black tigers, black foxes with long black fur and tails. There was a black mountain and there were black people. The gatekeeper of the Youdu city was a ferocious giant called Tu Bo, who had a tiger's head, three eyes and shining horns. And he pursued the weak spirits and ghosts of the city with great hands dripping blood.

The descendants of Hou Tu were a tribe of powerful giants who did not live in the city but on a wild mountain to the north. Their ancestor was Kua Fu. Even though they were ferocious-looking, with a snake hanging from each ear and a snake in each hand, they were said to be good-natured and kind, and not very intelligent.

One time Kua Fu was watching the sunset and he thought, "Each day the sun falls to earth leaving us in this hateful darkness. I will fix the sun in the sky so that we always have light."

With that he began to run in the direction of the setting sun, striding with his giant steps over mountains and rivers, as swift as the wind. Finally he came to a place called Yuyuan, or Yugu, which means "deep abyss", where the sun used to set.

He felt himself bathed in a bright red glow and stretched up his hand to grasp the red ball. But he was suddenly unbearably hot and thirsty. He rushed over to the Yellow River, lay down on his belly, and with a giant slurp swallowed up all the water. Still he was thirsty so he went and gulped up the Weishui River too. And still he was thirsty so he turned to go to Daze Lake in the north which is a thousand *li* across and the place where wild geese live and change their feathers each year. But Kua Fu, the poor giant who sought eternal light, never reached that lake. Weak and thirsty still, he died on the way, falling on to the ground, his eyes fixed on the last glow of the sun's twilight. Heavily, heavily his eyes fell closed and he slept for ever.

In the morning the sun rose as always in the east but the giant Kua Fu could not see it for he had turned into a mountain. On the north side of the mountain grew a thick grove of peach trees, which had sprung up from his walking stick. The delicious fruit of these trees would quench the thirst of anyone who passed by, and the place was called Kua Fu Mountain or Qinshan Mountain and is found today in the southeast of Henan Province.

The Final Defeat of Chi You

After the battle with the Yellow Emperor, Chi You's messengers arrived in the north at the home of the tribe Kua Fu, and they told those people all about the war and asked for help. Some giants didn't like war and refused to help, but others took up their cudgels to aid Chi You's defeated troops.

With the renewed strength of the giants, the morale of the rebel forces was revived, as though wings had been given to a tiger. Both sides were evenly matched again and the situation deadlocked once more. The Yellow Emperor saw that their battle would render no final decision, and so he decided to return to Xitai Mountain where he had first inspected the spirits and devils and incurred Chi You's proud disdain. There he spent three days and three nights meditating on how to deal with the rebels.

Suddenly in the sky before him appeared a goddess who looked like a bird with a human head. When the Yellow Emperor saw her, he knelt and dared not rise up again. The goddess said, "I am the Goddess of the Ninth Heaven. What would you like to ask me?"

And the Yellow Emperor answered, "My enemies have hidden themselves in the forests. Now I cannot conquer them and I fear that the lives of my troops, and of all my subjects, are in great

peril. Can you teach me new strategies, so that I can attack ten thousand times and win ten thousand battles?"

With a smile the goddess taught the Yellow Emperor new tactics such as heaven and earth had never seen before. And then she disappeared.

At that time too the Yellow Emperor made himself a precious new sword from the red copper of the Kunwu Mountains. It was green in colour and could cut iron and jade as if they were but lumps of soft earth.

Armed with new battle strategies and the powerful sword, the Yellow Emperor returned to his troops. In battle after battle they surprised Chi You's people. In the final skirmish, they laid seige to Chi You's army, which was now without magic powers and unable to escape. At that moment the dragon Ying Long flew through the sky, war drums thundered, and Kua Fu, the Miaos and all Chi You's brothers were slaughtered. So it was that Chi You's unhappy army descended to the underworld with masses of spirits mournfully entering into Youdu, the dark city.

As for Chi You himself, he was captured alive by the Yellow Emperor, who had no moment's thought of mercy towards the one whom he now considered the root of all earthly wrongdoing. Chi You was immediately sentenced to death, but even as the Yellow Emperor prepared to execute the sentence, he dared not unshackle Chi You for fear that the crafty one would escape. Not until his breath no longer mingled with the air of this world, not until there was no doubt at all that he was dead, did the Yellow Emperor remove the chains and throw them away into the wilderness. Later those same shackles changed into a forest of maple trees, and some people say that those red maples were dyed the colour of Chi You's blood.

But there are many accounts of the execution and burial of Chi You. Some say that the final battle was in Jizhou and that the Yellow Emperor cut off Chi You's head, burying it separately from the body for fear that they would join together again. The execution place was in Xie (now Xiexian County in Shanxi Province). At Juye the people called the burial place Jianbi, which means "body and limbs grave". The grave at Shouzhang, which is seven *zhang* tall, is thought to be the grave of Chi You's head. Pieces of his teeth were found near by. Every tenth lunar

month the ancient peoples gathered there to offer sacrifices and appease the god. Red clouds sometimes billowed out of the grave into the sky. The people called it Chi You's banner and interpreted it as a sign that Chi You would never in all eternity resign himself to the will of the great Yellow Emperor.

Xing Tian Takes Revenge: The Yellow Emperor's Last Battle

Xing Tian, which means "cut-off head", was an official of the Fiery Emperor in the south. The giant loved music and composed a piece called "Fuli" ("holding the plough") or "Fenglai" ("coming of phoenix") to honour his lord. He also loved poetry and composed the poem "Fengnian", which means "year of bumper harvest". He used his creativity to express his love for the land and the people of the south. He wanted to revenge the defeat of his Fiery Emperor, and when he heard the news of the bloody deaths of Chi You's brothers and the Miao people, the burning ember of hatred blazed up in his heart. He decided to challenge the Yellow Emperor personally and to fight until one of them lay dead.

So the giant set out from the south for the divine palace at the centre of the world. In his left hand he carried a shield, and in his right he carried an axe. Storming unexpectedly into the palace, he fought and killed the guards at each successive gate. There was none to equal him in power and fury along the way.

Word was rushed to the Yellow Emperor that the giant brute was coming. Flying into a rage, the god grasped his precious sword.

For a long time they fought. Into the clouds they fought. Down the side of the mountain they fought. From heaven to earth the battle raged, the axe chopping fiercely, the sword slashing swiftly. In a cloud of dust they fought to Changyang Mountain, when suddenly the Yellow Emperor saw the giant's axe falling over his head. Dodging to the side in a quick squat, he raised his sword to the giant's shoulder, and slashing sideways he sliced off his head. With a roar, the huge head thudded back heavily, eyes rolling, bloody mouth hanging agape. And then the head crashed to the ground like the thunders in the sky, shaking the valleys, and making the leaves tremble in the trees.

With horror, Xing Tian touched his shoulders to feel the hole where his head had been. Panicking, he shifted his axe to the other hand, squatted down, and began to flail around for his head. His giant left hand cut through the air, breaking trees and tossing away boulders until the sky was clouded with the debris of his search.

Watching the giant's fury, the Yellow Emperor feared his opponent would find his head and manage to put it back on his shoulders. So he raised the powerful sword and brought it down on the Changyang Mountain, slicing the mountain in two. Then he rolled the head into the gap and the mountain closed up again.

Hearing the crash, for a long moment the giant sat motionless, like a dark hill rooted to the earth for ten thousand years. His head was lost. He could not find his head. He could not see his victorious opponent. And he realized that his head had been hidden away from him for ever.

Desperately he sprang up. He began to heave his axe and shield in the empty air before him, randomly turning from side to side, storming against an unseen foe.

Some people say that Xing Tian used his two breasts for eyes and his navel for a mouth. His body became his head, and though his enemy had long since turned his back and returned home in victory, Xing Tian still fought there near the Changyang Mountain.

Like the little bird Jingwei, this headless one represents for the Chinese people the staunch, unyielding spirit of those early rebellions. The poet Tao Yuanming wrote a poem about him after reading his story in *Shanhaijing* (*Book of Mountains and Seas*).

Xing Tian raises high the axe and shield,
Ambitious, strong-willed for ever.

A Victory Celebration and the Gift of Silk

With the beheading of Xing Tian the long wars of the Yellow Emperor ended. To celebrate his victory he held an enormous banquet and composed a ten-part piece of music called "Ganggu". The titles of some of the pieces were "Leizhenjing" ("thundering fear"), "Menghuhai" ("surprise of the Fearful Tiger"), and "Diao'ezheng" ("battle between the Vultures and Kingfishers"). The banquet was magnificent, the soldiers singing and dancing, triumphant over their victory.

As they celebrated, a goddess descended from the heavens with a gift for the Yellow Emperor. Her body was covered with a horse's hide, and she presented two shining rolls of silk to the god. She was the "goddess of the silkworm", sometimes called the "lady with a horse's head". Long, long ago she had been a beautiful girl, but now a horse's skin grew over her body. If she pulled the two sides of the skin close to her body she became a silkworm with a horse's head, spinning a long, glittering thread of silk from her mouth. It is said she lived in a mulberry tree, producing silk day and night in the wild northern plain. This is her story.

Once in ancient times there lived a man, his daughter and their horse. Often the man had to travel, leaving his daughter alone at home to take care of the beast. And often the girl was lonely. One day, because she missed her father she teased the horse: "Dear long-nosed one, if you could bring my father home right now, I'd marry you and be your wife." At that the horse broke out of his harness. He galloped away and came quickly to the place where the master was doing business. The master, surprised to see his beast, grasped his mane and jumped up on his back. The horse stood mournfully staring in the direction he had come from, so the man decided there must be something amiss at home and hurried back.

When they arrived home, the daughter explained that she had only remarked that she missed her father and the horse had dashed off wildly. The man said nothing but was secretly pleased to own such a remarkable animal and fed him special sweet hay. But the horse would not touch it and whinnied and reared each time he saw the girl.

The man began to worry about the horse's strange behaviour, and one day he said to the girl, "Why is it that our horse behaves so strangely whenever you are about?"

So the young girl confessed the teasing remark she had made.

When he heard this the father was enraged, "For shame to say such a thing to an animal! No one must know of this! You will stay locked in the house!"

Now the man had always liked this horse, but he would not hear of its becoming his son-in-law. That night, to prevent any more trouble, he crept quietly into the stable with his bow and arrow and shot the horse through the heart. Then he skinned it and hung up the hide in the courtyard.

Next day, when the father was away, the girl ran out of the house to join some other children playing in the courtyard near the horse hide. When she saw it she kicked it angrily and said, "Dirty horse hide! What made you think such an ugly long-snouted creature as you could become my . . ."

But before she could finish, the hide suddenly flew up and wrapped itself around her, swift as the wind, and carried her away out of sight. The other children watched dumbfounded; there was nothing they could do but wait to tell the old man when he arrived home.

Her father set out immediately in search of his daughter, but in vain. Some days later a neighbouring family found the girl wrapped up in the hide in the branches of a mulberry tree. She had turned into a wormlike creature spinning a long thread of shining silk from her horse-shaped head, spinning it round and round her in a soft cocoon.

Such is the story of the goddess of the silkworm. The Yellow Emperor was delighted to receive her exquisite gift of silk at his celebration banquet. The cloth was as light and filmy as wispy clouds in the sky, shining as clear spring water in a mountain stream. He ordered his official tailor, Bo Yu, to create new ceremonial robes and hats. And Lei Zu, the revered queen mother of gods and people, wife of the Emperor, began then to collect silkworms and grow them. And so it was that the Chinese people learned of silk.

Now that the Yellow Emperor had conquered the tribes of Chi You and chopped off the head of Xing Tian, he was victorious but still not safe against rebellion. He tried to kill all the Miao people, but they were resilient like dry autumn weeds on the wild plain which even fire cannot destroy: as soon as spring comes, they burst into life again. At a later time when his great-grandson Zhuan Xu took the throne, those Miaos rose to prosperity once more, and fearing that they would disturb heaven's peace, the Emperor cut off the way between heaven and earth. So ended the wars between heaven and earth, though bloody battles between the Miaos and human emperors continued.

The Flowering of Culture

When there is relative peace in a nation, only then can true joy and inventions of the imagination flourish. After the wars with Chi You were ended, the Yellow Emperor fathered a period of growth. Some say he created ships and carts; some say he cast twelve great mirrors. He was said to have taught the people how to build houses to protect themselves against the rain, how to use pots and pans for cooking. He invented arrows and playing balls; with his four-eyed official Cang Ji he created writing. He asked Lin Lun to formulate the structure of music, and Lei Gong (Duke of Thunder) and Qi Bo to write medical books. The Yellow Emperor thus became master of all powers. He travelled the world with his assistant Feng Hou carrying his books and Chang Bo carrying his precious sword. They left their marks in many places during these voyages.

The Yellow Emperor ordered his officials to collect copper from the Shoushan Mountain to cast at the foot of the Jingshan Mountain a huge three-legged bronze cooking vessel in commemoration of his victory over Chi You. Flying dragons, gods, demons and animals all intertwined over the surface of that great vessel, alive with the vision of the Yellow Emperor. He displayed it at Jingshan Mountain and invited a great company of gods and earthly princes to come and view it.

The Yellow Emperor Returns to Heaven

As they were viewing the great copper pot, there appeared in the sky a divine dragon covered with golden scales. It drew half its body out of the clouds, its long beard dropping down and brushing the great vessel. The Yellow Emperor recognized his servant, sent to bring him back to the heavenly palace. With more than seventy officials he climbed on to the back of the dragon and floated up into the sky. Many of the immortals who were gathered there wanted to go with them, but there was no more room on the dragon's back. They tried to hold on to his beard, but so many hung there that the beard broke, and everyone tumbled back crying out their misfortune. Now people say that the plant called "dragon-beard grass" first grew from the bits of beard those gods pulled out.

So it was that the gods and people lived separately, and the gods seldom thought any more about the life they had left behind on earth.

Among those gods who were not able to return to the heavens were two who were so unfortunate because, some say, they were made too mortal by the warring on earth. One of these was Ba, the Yellow Emperor's own daughter. She still gave off enormous heat, and wherever she lived followed drought, dry clouds, and not a drop of rain. She was welcomed by no one and was called Han (Dry) Ba. Later, Shu Jun, a niece of Hou Yi (ancestor of the Zhou nation), informed the Yellow Emperor, and so he arranged for Dry Ba to live in the north of Chishui River. But occasionally she grew lonely, and wandering south she brought drought. The people would dig a ditch and chant:

> *Oh goddess, oh goddess,*
> *return to the north.*
> *Return to Chishui,*
> *that is your home.*

She would be ashamed to hear this song and would return to her home.

Ying Long the dragon was another god left behind, even though he had accomplished many valiant deeds for the Supreme Emperor during the greatest battles with Chi You. It seems the Yellow Emperor forgot him. Silently he moved south and lived there in the cool mountain pools. Ying Long was a rain-gatherer and gave his gift to the south wherever there was drought. The people used to dress and dance like dragons, praying for renewal, praying for the fresh rains of Ying Long.

So it was that the immortals left some of their company behind, but the time of their long stay on earth was finally over and the great ancient gods disappeared into the heavens for ever.

Chapter 4
DIVINE HEROES

Two Gods of the Yin Nation

When the Yin nation was conquered by the Zhou people, the stories of the gods began to blend together. However, we know from the records that certain gods were originally Yin, and so we present their stories together here. The stories of two gods of the east, Di Jun and Di Ku, are often interchangeable, and it would seem that these two gods eventually became one. They are particularly important because many of their stories are concerned with origins; origins of either a certain people or a certain state.

Di Jun

Although there are few stories about Di Jun, we know that he liked to amuse himself with five-coloured birds. He kept three kinds of mythical birds: *wang*, *luan*, and *feng*. Like the phoenix, they liked to eat fruits and their appearance on earth was a sign of peace.

Di Jun had three wives. The first was E Wang, who lived in a place called "Three Bodies" and gave birth to three-bodied people. These people were called Yao. They ate five grains: rice, wheat, beans and two kinds of millet. They kept leopards, tigers and bears as servants. But Di Jun's other two wives were even more important. The first was Xi He, the mother of the ten suns, who lived in the Ganyuan abyss beyond the southeast sea. Xi He helped the suns bathe, one by one, with clear spring waters, which made them shine brilliantly to hang in the sky. The last wife was called Chang Xi. She lived in the west and bore twelve daughters who were the moons.

There are several records of Di Jun's descendants. It is said that Di Jun governed four states with different kinds of people: Zhangyong, Siyou, Baimin and Heichi. The Siyou people divided into a male group called Sishi (hoping for boys) and a female group called Sinu (hoping for girls). These people didn't need husbands or wives but could have children all alone; they simply needed to fix their eyes on each other for a moment.

The people of the west plain were also thought to be Di Jun's descendants. His sons in the west were Hou Ji, who brought new crops to earth, and Tai Er, whose son Shu Jun learned to manage the crops and tame wild oxen to plough the fields. It was Shu Jun's descendants who later became the Western Zhou state.

Di Jun had several other descendants whose achievements survive in the fragments: Fan Yu, who created ships; Ji Guang, who created the wood cart; and Yan Long, who invented the lovely stringed instrument called *qinse*.

Di Ku

Di Ku

The most famous story from Di Ku's time is the story of Fang Wang's rebellion. Since Di Ku was sometimes also called Fang, it is likely that this is the story of a conflict between his two sons. The reigning title of the other son was King Gao Xin. The importance of this tale is that it is an account of the origins of certain southern minority groups.

Once during the reign of King Gao Xin, the queen developed a painful ear disease. She consulted wise healers, but no one knew what was the matter. Finally after three years had passed, a golden worm, three inches long, was plucked from her ear. Now as soon as the worm was pulled out, the queen had no more problems, so she put the worm in a basket and fed it and let it grow. She watched it stretch to a length of two *zhang* (about twenty feet) and change into an enormous dragon dog covered with coloured scales. The king, most impressed, called the creature Pan Hu and kept it as his pet dog.

Now in those days the emperor was troubled with a rebellious army whose leader Fang Wang he could not defeat. After many battles he declared to his officials, "If anyone can bring me Fang Wang's head, I will give him my daughter, the princess, to marry."

Most of the men had already fought the powerful Fang Wang

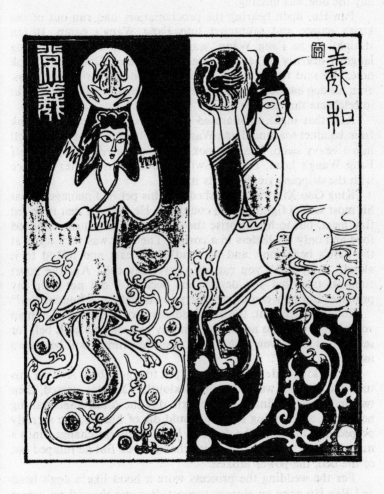

and dared not risk their lives, even for such a prize. But from that day the dog was missing.

Pan Hu, upon hearing the proclamation, had run out of the king's palace and sauntered into Fang Wang's camp. It ran straight up to Fang Wang, wagging its tail, and Fang Wang laughed heartily to see the dog of his enemy Gao Xin. "Look here," he said to his men, "Gao Xin is bound for failure; now even his dog has deserted. Let everyone come to a banquet tonight to celebrate this good omen."

And that night, exhilarated with self-confidence and drunk from banquet toasting, Fang Wang stumbled into his tent and fell into a heavy sleep. The dog took its chance, crept in, and bit off Fang Wang's head, running swiftly back to its master's palace with the dripping trophy in its mouth.

King Gao Xin was astonished that his pet had managed what his most skilful fighting men could not. He ordered that it be fed fine meat, but to his surprise the dog would not touch the good food and only lay listless in a corner. The king was very upset at the hero's behaviour, and he fondled its ears and talked to it aloud: "Why don't you eat, or answer my call? Are the court rumours true that you despise me because I did not keep my promise? But how can a dog marry my daughter, a human girl?"

To his amazement, the dog suddenly spoke out with a human voice: "My king, do not worry. Simply put me in a gold bell for seven days and seven nights, and after that time I will become a man."

So the king ordered the animal put in a gold bell. And all this time the princess was watching anxiously. One day passed, then two and three . . . finally on the sixth day she could stand waiting no longer, and fearing the dog would die of hunger, she secretly peeped into the bell. The dog Pan Hu had almost changed into a man. Only its head was not quite changed yet. But he jumped out of the bell, the power broken.

For the wedding the princess wore a hood like a dog's head and Pan Hu wore an elegant topcoat. Because the girl no longer wanted to live at court with her dog-headed husband, Pan Hu took his new wife to Nanshan, the southern mountains, and they settled in a cave. They lived happily there and had three sons and a daughter.

After some time they worried that none of these children had a surname and so they asked the king to give them names. The king decided to issue an edict about their names. He called the eldest Pan (tray) for he was put into a tray after his birth. The second was called Lan (basket) for he was kept in a basket. The king thought and thought and could not come up with a surname for the third son. But as he was thinking, some thunder rolled outside his window and so the child was called Lei, which means "thunder". The daughter took the name of her young husband, a brave soldier called Zhong. These three sons and the daughter had many children and created a new state, of which the honoured ancestor was the dog Pan Hu.

Di Ku's Music

When Di Ku ruled as an emperor on earth he loved music and did many things to develop it. He had Xian Hei, one of his officials, compose certain songs: Jiuzhao, Liuying and Liulie. He also asked You Chui to make eight different kinds of musical instruments: the *pigu* (a small drum), the *zhong* (a kind of bell), the *ling* (an inverted bell), the *guan* (a flute), the *xun* (an egg-shaped clay wind instrument with six holes), the *chi* (a bamboo flute with eight holes), the *tao* (a drum-shaped rattle), and the *zhui zhong* (also a kind of bell). Besides the new sounds created by these instruments, the emperor asked the phoenixes called Tiandi to open their wings and dance in the imperial hall.

Di Ku's Wives and Ancestors

In one tale Di Ku had a concubine called Zou Tu, who dreamed eight times that she ate a sun in the sky. After each dream she gave birth to a human son. We notice here the strong connection the god of the east always has with the sun. In another account Di Ku had four wives. Their names were Jiang Yuan, who gave birth to Hou Ji; Jian Di, whose son was Qi; Qing Du, whose son became King Yao; and finally Chang Xi, who bore Di Zhi, successor to Yao's throne.

We present here two stories, one about Qi, ancestor of the Yin state, and one about Hou Ji, ancestor of the Zhou state.

Qi

To create a peaceful alliance, King Gao Xin married Jian Di and Jian Pi, two daughters of the powerful tribe of Yousong in the north. He loved them and built them a nine-storey terrace to live on and ordered drums and bells to amuse them while they ate. Once the king sent them a swallow, and the girls were amused and caught it in a jade basket with a handkerchief. But when they lifted the cloth, the bird escaped, leaving two eggs behind. Jian Di ate the eggs and gave birth to Qi. Others say she was taking a bath in the river with two other ladies when a swallow passed by and dropped an egg which she immediately ate.

Her son's name, Qi, means "open", since it is said that at birth he opened his mother's bosom. When he grew up, he was administrator in charge of education and helped Yu to regulate the rivers. He was the ancestor of the Yin state, and some people remember him as Xuan Wang, King of Swallows.

Hou Ji

Now Jiang Yuan, first wife of Di Ku, was said to have been married a long time without having a child. This troubled her deeply.

One day as she was walking she saw a huge footprint, and placing her own foot in the print, she immediately felt a strange shiver run through her body. Not long after, she discovered she was pregnant, and she gave birth to a boy. But she was ashamed to have such a child and left him in a lane where cows and sheep cared for him and gave him milk to drink. When the people saw that he was still alive, they threw him into a forest, but some peasants working there brought him back. Finally the child was left on the ice of a frozen plain. Thousands of birds descended from the sky to protect and warm him. The people were amazed and believed they had seen a sign, so they rescued the child and called him Qi, a name meaning "the discarded". Later people called him Hou Ji.

Hou Ji became an excellent farmer and produced wheat, millet, beans, rice, sorghum and wild melons. He made simple farm tools, and later King Yao asked him to guide the people in agriculture. His brother Tai Xi and nephew Shun Jun were also good farmers. Hou Ji left a colourful stone called the "Five-Crop Stone" that produced many foods. When Hou Ji died, the people buried him on Duguang Plain, a beautiful place of rivers and hills where you could see the heavenly ladder on which the gods descended to earth.

King Yao

Yao was the first king of the legendary states. He was considered to be a great king because he led a simple, hard-working life, never living any better than the doorkeepers of his court. In summer he wore sackcloth and in winter only a deerskin. His century-long reign was plagued with disasters —droughts, floods, starvation and terrible suffering. But despite these hardships, his deep concern for his subjects remained constant. If a man had no clothes Yao said, "It is I who fail to clothe him." If the people were starving he blamed himself for their suffering. And when someone committed a crime Yao said, "I am the source of this crime."

Auspicious Signs and Inventions

King Yao's kingdom was considered the most peaceful of the legendary period. Yao was not only well-loved by the people but seemed to have been well-favoured by the gods. Such auspicious signs as his horses' straw turning to rice and the appearance of a phoenix in his yard occurred during his reign. Many ingenious inventions are also attributed to Yao. One of the most interesting was the first imperial calendar, a plant called the *mingjia* or *lijia*. Each day for fifteen days the plant sprouted a bean. Then one bean would fall to the ground each day. On those months with only twenty-nine days, the last bean hung and withered on the plant.

Yao's Officials

A peaceful state is reflected in the king's choice of his officials. Yao's officials were known for their remarkable backgrounds, skills and wisdom. He chose Hou Ji, descendant of the god of the east, to be official of agriculture, and Chui, known as a most skilful craftsman, to be official of engineering. The strategist Qi was made leader of the army; and wise Shun, official of education. Yao's official of music, Kui, was thought to have had only one leg. Some say from his appearance that he was a descendant of the Kui cow in Liuposhan in the eastern sea. He could calm the hottest tempers and make even the birds and animals dance to his divine music. His most famous composition was the beautiful "Da Zhang", which he composed from the sounds he heard in the mountain streams and deep forested valleys.

Finally there was Gao Tao, minister of justice. Gao Tao was known for his sternness but also for his fair judgement despite his strange methods. He was a peculiar-looking judge with a horse's mouth and a face as green as the surface of a watermelon. He kept at his side a divine single-horned sheep called Xie Zhi. The sheep's body was as large as a bear's and covered with long green wool. It liked to live near water in the summer and deep in the pine forest in winter. It helped in judging all the most difficult cases; if the accused were guilty, the sheep would strike the wrongdoer with its horn, but when the accused was innocent, the sheep remained as still as stone. Thus, Gao Tao was always fair and accurate in his judgements.

Famous Gifts

During the late period of Yao's kingdom, the state of Zhizhi sent him a bird with double eyeballs. It was a precious bird which looked like a cock, cried like a phoenix, and had extraordinary powers. It could pull off all its feathers and fly naked into the sky. The bird was capable of fighting beasts of prey and had the power to drive away evil spirits. It ate nothing but a magical jade mixture, softened into a delicate pastry. Only occasionally did the bird appear—sometimes several times a year, sometimes not for years on end. But the people liked it and cleaned their homes and streets in its honour. Later, people carved an image of the bird to hang in front of their doors because it was said to have the power to drive away evil spirits.

Yao lived a rigorous life, and his health was sometimes poor. But at that time there lived in Huaishan Mountain an old man called Wo Quan who gathered herbs. As he picked fairy herbs from the mountainside, his body became covered with white hair and his eyes grew into cubes. Aged though he was, he was strong as an ox and swift as a horse. Hearing that the favourite king was sickly, he felt pity and gathered special pine seeds from the mountains to offer Yao, giving him careful eating instructions. But the good King Yao was too busy to remember to take his herb for longevity. It is said that some others took it and lived to be three hundred years old, but Yao himself only lived for a hundred years.

Respect for the King

There are some who despise the post of a minister and a fief of a thousand chariots, content with vegetable broth in a narrow lane. Since even human beings have such different standards, Heaven must differ even more. (Han Yu, in *Records of the Historian*.)

There are several humorous anecdotes about Yao's benevolent tolerance of the different opinions of his subjects. Chinese readers consider the following two stories to be quite humorous in their obvious acceptance of points of view differing from the king's. The first points out false humility and the second satirizes ignorance.

One time when Yao was already old he decided to choose a wise man to succeed him. He would not consider his own son, Dan Zhu, whom he thought too weak to lead the people. As he searched he was told everywhere that Xu You in Yangcheng was the man he should choose. So Yao went personally to Xu You's house.

But Xu You was aloof during the king's visit. He said that he was not interested in being king, and fearing that he would be pressed into service, he ran away that night to live by the Yinshui River in the Jishan Mountains. Yao was disheartened but still felt that Xu You could do the best job. So he sent some of his officials to ask him again to govern the nine counties. Xu You did not want to hear these proposals and went to the river to wash his ears.

Just as he was dipping his second ear into the water, his friend Chao Fu came by to water his cow. Puzzled by his friend's strange behaviour, Chao Fu asked Xu You what he was doing and heard this reply: "King Yao wants to offer me a post. But I so hate to hear these dirty words that I am washing them away."

But the friend Chao Fu just laughed at this arrogance and said, "Enough nonsense! I would sympathize, my friend, if you had lived secluded in the mountains all your life seeking anonymity—for then who would come to trouble you? But you did not follow such a path. Rather, you went into the world and made for yourself a reputation. Only arrogance makes you wash your ears, so stop dirtying the water and my poor cow's mouth."

And with this he led his cow further upstream to drink.

Another time, during a brief period of peace, an old man was playing *ji rang*, a game with sharpened sticks. The people observing his great skill called out and praised him: "Wonderful! The virtues of the king shine through this old man."

But the old man replied, "I don't know what you mean! I get up early in the morning to work and I go to bed late at night. I drink the water I draw from my own well and eat the food grown in my own fields. What kindness do I know from the king?"

And he went on playing his game skilfully while the observers stood silent, unable to answer his question.

Yao's Evil Son, Dan Zhu

Yao had ten sons, the eldest of whom was a proud and tyrannical man called Dan Zhu. During the time of the floods, while Yao and the people suffered, Dan Zhu cared nothing for them—he was bad-tempered and used the disaster to travel great distances by boat. He made men row, and when the rivers were shallow he forced them to push and pull the vessel along.

Yao, of course, worried about Dan Zhu, who argued often with his nine brothers. It was impossible to offer the kingship to such a man, and so he made up his mind to offer the power to a loyal subject named Shun. But Yao feared that his eldest son would resent this and make trouble, so he sent him to be duke under Hou Ji in the south.

King Yao was not mistaken in his judgement of his son. As soon as Dan Zhu learned of Yao's decision, he gathered three tribes called the Sanmiao to rebel against his father. The Sanmiao were easily defeated by Yao's troops, and Dan Zhu and his followers headed south. But a rash son, humiliated and defeated by his father, will not wait long to seek revenge. Again they battled and again the son was defeated.

In deep humiliation, Dan Zhu drowned himself in the South Sea. His sorrowful father asked the people living in that area to offer sacrifices to him once a year. And so those people stayed at that place in the state, calling themselves Sanmiao.

The Heritage of King Yao

Although today the Yellow Emperor is generally considered to be the original god and ancestor of the Chinese people, stories of King Yao often appear in accounts of ancient origins. The stories merge allowing a diversity of allusion concerning beginnings. So it is that the Tang Dynasty poet Sikong Tu can perceive both figures as immortal ancestors.

Above Mount Hua the night is blue,
And men hear the clear toll of a bell . . .
Stand then apart in purity of heart,
Break through the confines of mortality,
Aloof as the Yellow Emperor and Yao,
Alone at the source of the Great Mystery.

Shun, Yao's Successor

Almost as well-loved as Yao was his sucessor Shun. It was during their two reigns that the great flood was conquered and many improvements made for the people. When Shun finally died, his wives drowned on a mourning trip for him and were turned into river nymphs. Their tears sank into a bamboo forest and they were commemorated by the poet Li He:

On lonely hills the clouds freeze and are still.
The river nymphs weep in their bamboo grove.

Shun's Birth and Marriage

There was once a blind peasant called Gu Sou who dreamed that a phoenix carried rice to him. It said: "My name is Ji and I will be your child."

Not too long after the strange dream, the blind man's wife gave birth to a child. His name was Shun, and people say that Shun looked different. He had two pupils in each eye, and because of this he was also called Chong Hua.

The child's mother died soon after, and the blind man married again to a woman who had a son named Xiang and a daughter named Xi. But the coming of this woman and her children disturbed the harmony of the household. The blind man favoured the children of his new wife; the whole family turned against Shun, and only his stepsister occasionally showed him kindness.

The poor boy suffered many beatings, both from his parents and from his cruel stepbrother. When his suffering grew too great, he ran to his mother's grave and wept.

His stepmother wished young Shun dead, a wish she made widely known, and finally the boy could stand his pain no longer. He ran away to a place at the foot of Lishan Mountain near the Guishui River. There he built himself a small hut and cultivated some land. Sometimes at twilight after a hard day's toil in the fields he would sit and watch mother birds flying with their young, singing in the trees, and he would mourn for his good mother. From the depths of his loneliness he began to sing.

The virtue and sadness of Shun touched the hearts of the people near Guishui. The peasants offered him land, and that land flourished. When he went to Lake Leize, the fishermen showed him the good fishing spots. When he went to Hebin to learn to make pottery, everyone's earthenware became more beautiful. The people loved Shun; they welcomed him into their homes because wherever he went, the place became more prosperous. So by the time he was only twenty, Shun was a famous man.

It was just at that time that King Yao was searching for a wise man to succeed him, and all the people suggested Shun. Yao was pleased to find such a man. He offered Shun two wives, his daughters, E Huang and Nu Ying, and he asked his nine sons to live near by to judge the competence of Shun. He gave Shun new clothes, a new musical instrument, *qin*, and cows and sheep, and asked the people to build storehouses for Shun's crops.

So it was that Shun, the abandoned child and solitary peasant, became the son-in-law of King Yao. Everyone respected him except his father's family. They hated him all the more, their hatred fuelled by jealousy.

But Shun was the kind of man who knows no such jealousy and hatred. According to custom, a married man must take his wife to his father's house, and son Shun took his wives home with many presents. With humility the two young women served their new parents, trying to dispel the hatred of the blind man's family.

Xiang Tries to Murder Shun

Not long after Shun and his wives arrived, the family began to plot against him. His father and stepmother wanted his wealth, his stepbrother wanted his wives. Only the stepsister wanted nothing, though she stood by watching them plot.

One evening the stepbrother went to Shun's house and called through the window, "Brother, Father asks that you come and help repair the storehouse tomorrow. Be there early."

Shun was working in the courtyard and called back gently, "Of course, I'll be there."

His wives E Huang and Nu Ying came out of the house and asked what their brother-in-law had wanted. When Shun told them, his wives looked troubled and said, "We fear you will be in danger. We think they are plotting to burn you."

Shun did not know what to do. How could he refuse his father? But E Huang and Nu Ying thought about it and finally said, "Never mind then, go as you planned. But you must not wear those old clothes. We'll give you some new clothes to wear."

The two sisters had learned the arts of the fairies, and they knew how to predict the future and make magic weapons. With wisdom and good hearts they sought to protect their husband, so when Shun set off next day, he was clad in a colourful feathery cloak.

The family had made ready a trap for Shun. They pretended to greet him kindly, and they brought a ladder for him to climb to the top of the broken storehouse. Honest Shun began his work and didn't notice the family piling straw inside. Nor did he see them take away his ladder. When suddenly he glanced down, he called out: "What are you doing?"

And his cruel stepmother called up: "We are sending you to heaven to meet your own wretched mother," and Shun heard his blind father's foolish laughter echo her words.

A torch was lit, and his stepbrother cast it into the dry straw. The flames leapt up and Shun called for help. His body dripped with sweat, and as the fire roared closer, ready to swallow him up, he threw open his arms and yielded, calling out, "Oh, my dear mother in heaven!"

At that moment his feathery cloak was transformed into wings which flew away into the sky, carrying Shun above the flames.

So it was that the first plot came to nothing, but the family would not give up their awful ambitions. Some time later, Shun's father himself came to his son to apologize and ask forgiveness. Shun received him graciously and agreed to help the family work on a well the next morning.

After the blind man had left, Shun told his wives, who said: "They will try to hurt you again. But don't worry, we will help you."

So once again Shun was given a new set of clothes, this time scaly like a dragon's skin. He was told to wear them under his old coat and, if anything happened, to take off the outer clothes.

This time when Shun came to the house, where the family was beginning to work on the well, they were glad to see that he had no special clothing. Shun gathered the tools he would need; then slowly they lowered him down into the gloom on a hemp swing. But hardly had Shun reached the bottom when he felt the rope snap and earth and stones begin to shower down on his head. Shun had learned his lesson. Immediately he ripped off his coat, and his clothes turned him into a golden dragon that ducked down into the underground stream and swam out of another well. So Shun had already escaped when his family finished filling the well with earth and stones. They sang triumphantly at the young man's death, and together they went to his home to steal his possessions and his wives. Even the sister Xi followed them.

At the news of Shun's death his two wives were in despair. That artful brother Xiang began to divide the property, claiming the largest portion as his own.

"I will take the instrument, Shun's bow and arrows, and his wives," said Xiang, his voice black with greed. "Mother and father will have the sheep and cows, the house and fields ... Hey! You two women! Come here and look upon the face of your new husband!"

The sister Xi flushed with deep shame as she watched the grief of the two wives and the greed of her parents as they rooted through the dead man's possessions. She began to weep, thinking of how she might have saved her unsuspecting brother.

Suddenly the family felt a presence in the doorway. They whirled around in shock to see Shun himself standing there watching the scene.

At last the stepbrother gathered his wits to say, "Why Shun, I was just thinking of you, much troubled indeed."

Grimly Shun answered, "I know you were thinking of me."

And no further word was uttered. Despite their cruelty, Shun's tolerance of his family remained; only his stepsister changed, and she began to love her elder brother and sisters-in-law with all her heart.

But the brother Xiang remained devious. One evening sister Xi heard her family devising yet another scheme, and so she hurried over to her brother's home and told his wives.

Next morning Xiang came to the house and said: "Brother, we are truly sorry for the way we have mistreated you. Please forgive us and honour our house with your presence at a banquet tomorrow night."

Shun was troubled and discussed the matter with his wives, who already knew all about it. The elder woman said: "Go in confidence, my husband. We know how to deal with your family."

The younger wife then returned with a small bag of medicine. "Take this," she instructed, "and mix it with dog dung into your bath water. Then bathe in it just before you go to dinner."

Next evening Shun did as he was instructed and then set out for his parents' home. The family received Shun as their honoured guest, placing plate after plate of delicacies before him. All evening they toasted him, keeping his wine cup full. And according to the custom, Shun emptied his glass with every toast. Indeed, the house rang with festivity, but behind the door waited a carefully placed, razor-sharp axe.

Shun drank cup after cup of wine. Even the other members of the family began to feel drunk, but Shun was sober as stone. As soon as the bottles were emptied and the food all gone, Shun rose and, thanking them gravely for the banquet, went out of the door and returned to his home.

Shun Is Offered the Kingdom

Yao was now informed by his nine sons and two daughters of Shun's family loyalty and of his benevolence and wisdom. He wished only to see Shun's abilities for himself. He devised a series of tests and invited Shun to the palace to act as official of trade.

For a first test, Shun was sent to a thick mountain forest in an area known for its terrible thunderstorms. Shun feared nothing in the forest. Poisonous snakes slithered away from him, wild animals returned to their lairs and caves. The thunders came, lightning flashed through the sky, and the heavy winds and rain whipped tall trees from side to side. The forest was a blind, wailing darkness, yet brave Shun managed to find his way out. The other tests have been lost or forgotten, but some records report that Shun was helped in all his tasks by his wives. And by the end of these tests Yao was convinced and handed over his power to Shun.

Other Tales of Shun

The records hold many other fragmentary tales about the goodness of Shun. Some say that after he was made king, Shun returned to Guishui to visit his blind father and offer his brother Xiang the title of duke. It is said that the family was amazed at his magnanimity and began to change their natures.

Like Yao, in his later years, King Shun felt that his own eldest son, Shang Jun, who loved only singing and dancing, could not be a good leader. Rather he offered his power to Yu, who had conquered the flood and regulated the rivers.

At the end of Shun's reign he made many inspection tours and died on such a trip in the southern wilderness of Cangwu. When people heard the news, they mourned as if for their own parents. His two wives, who had shared so many years and ordeals with their husband, set out mourning on a long southward voyage, meeting many peoples and seeing many strange sights. They shed tears all the way; their tears sank into the ground like earth springs to become the deep-rooted bamboo forest. These bamboo still grow in Hunan Province and are called *xiangfei* or teardrop bamboo. The poor devoted wives drowned in a shipwreck while trying to cross the Xiangshui River, and they turned into river goddesses. People say they can sometimes be seen there still, drifting over the surface of the waves.

Shun was buried deep in the Jiuyi Mountains south of Cangwu. He was buried among nine valleys and twisting streams in a place that most people cannot find. They say that some have entered there, a maze from which few escape.

So lies the hero Shun, quite alone in death, protected by the flowing rivers, hidden by the deep mountain valleys.

Yi, the Archer

Chang E, remorseful for having stolen the elixir,
Nightly pines amid the vast sea of the blue sky.

Li Shangyin (813–858)

In the ancient records there is no single continuous story of Yi. The story of how he shot the ten suns and how his wife, Chang E, flew to the moon is familiar throughout China. Yi lived during the reign of Yao, not long after the Yellow Emperor. Some fragments say that he was banished from the heavens, and

because Chang E was his wife, she too was exiled to the earth.
Their story is recorded in *Shanhaijing* and is discussed by
Mencius.

The Ten Strange Suns

During the reign of King Yao, ten suns mysteriously appeared
in the heaven, bringing near disaster to the king and his people.
The sky was a blinding world of suns; no shadow could be found
on earth. The crops withered in the searing heat. The stones began
to melt. And the people could barely breathe. They soon found
almost nothing to eat and feared starvation.

These ten suns were the sons of Di Jun, god of the east, and
his wife, Xi He. Their home was in the boiling Eastern Sea called
Yanggu. They lived on Fusang, an enormous tree which towered
a thousand *zhang* into the air from the depths of those boiling
waters.

This tree had nine branches along its trunk and a special
branch at the very top. Before the great disaster, one of those suns
would rise to the top branch each day to begin the voyage over
the earth, while his nine brothers waited below.

Each day their mother prepared a flying cart drawn by six
dragons. First the boy washed himself in the boiling sea, then
mounted the dragon cart and rose to the top of the Fusang tree.
Each day the dragon cart traced exactly the same path through
the sky. The top of the Fusang tree was called Chenming
(early dawn). At the place Feiming (beginning dawn) the freshly
washed new sun mounted his dragon cart to begin his voyage
across the sky. By the time he was seen on earth he had already
travelled to Danming (complete dawn). And so the passage of the
sun each day was very regular.

Usually the mother accompanied her son only as far as
Beichuan. There she would stop her cart and let her son fly
across the sky alone while she returned. Sometimes though, she
accompanied him the entire way and together they reached the
western abyss called Yuyuan. Mother Xi He remained there
with her son until the last rays of twilight disappeared in the
Menggu Sea; then she hurried back to Yanggu to bathe and

prepare her next son for his journey the following morning.

Until this time, the heat and the light on earth had been orderly—enough to grow crops, keep people warm, and preserve the land and rivers. Day in, day out, with the help of their mother, the ten suns carried out her plan.

But one night, left alone to their own devices, these ten suns began to talk in the hot darkness of the Fusang tree. Did they dare to break out of the interminable boredom of their mother's cart? Debating till dawn, drunk with their heated talk, they rushed with one will away from Yanggu, kicking over their mother's cart. Suddenly free, they burst joyfully into the sky and danced above the earth. They vowed to remain united and strong, rising and sinking together each day, never parting from one another.

But the suffering people below, burning and hungry, could not endure the suns' rebellion. King Yao was deeply troubled by this new disaster and, according to the custom of the time, he invited Nu Chou, the most powerful sorceress of the state, to perform her magic arts, to pray for rains and drive away the suns.

Early in the morning people began to prepare for the witch's arrival. She was said to wander the earth on a one-horned dragon-fish. She kept a giant crab slave and was able to stand on the clouds to fly across the sky. When she finally arrived that morning, she was wearing a green skirt like Han Ba, the daughter of the Yellow Emperor. People beat drums, chanted and prayed. Atop the altar Nu Chou prayed with all her powers. Drumming and praying, chanting and wailing echoed eerily through the night darkness.

But still the suns rose up.

The praying people hurried to hide beneath any scrap of shade, leaving the witch alone and exposed on the stone altar. From the shadows they peeked out, watching. Sweat poured from her glowing skin, rolling down her body. She gasped for air and held up her wide sleeves to shade her head. She swayed away from the altar as if drunk, her powerful magic useless. Some people rushed out to rescue her, but she crumpled to the earth, struck dead already by those ten mighty suns.

Nu Chou's death created great despair among the people. The disaster of the ten suns was spreading to every corner of the earth;

hungry beasts of prey pressed out of the hot forests and boiling rivers, devouring the people. And so those people grieved. And so they suffered.

King Yao no longer knew what to do. If his people suffered, he suffered ten thousand times for every one of them. He turned to Di Jun, god of the east, praying and helpless.

Day after day Di Jun heard King Yao's petition. The god dared not raise his hand against his own sons. But he saw the earth's disaster and could not ignore King Yao's entreaties. So he asked his official Yi to go down to earth to help the good King Yao.

Now Yi was a small god in the heaven, but an especially accomplished archer. He could shoot the tiny speck of a sparrow flying swiftly in a distant sky. Yi's fame spread wide, and even those who knew nothing of archery were proud to hold Yi's quiver. Di Jun gave Yi a new red bow and a quiver of white arrows and sent him with his beautiful, strong-willed wife, Chang E, to stop the destruction of those rebellious suns.

He said to Yi: "Go you now down to earth and put an end to these wrongdoings. Threaten my sons with this bow."

So Yi left the Heavenly Palace, taking with him Chang E. On earth they hurried immediately to King Yao in his stifling hut; he received them with great joy. Together they made a tour of the land. Yi was horrified to see emaciated people half burnt, moaning with thirst from thick, blackened lips on the sterile land. Weakly they reached out to their king and the strange archer who walked by his side. Yi's strong hands trembled at the sight of such misery. And he pitied them, and was furious at the rebel suns.

But in that moment of rage Yi forgot the god's exacting words: "Threaten those suns with this bow." He could think of nothing but destroying them all.

Yi stood out on the open plain, a group of people gathered around him to watch. He tightened his bowstring and counted ten arrows in his quiver. He stretched his powerful arms and, slowly raising his bow, paused and squinted up at the suns. An arrow streaked through the air and suddenly one of those suns silently cracked and split. Brilliant sparks and golden feathers burst into the air like some strange celestial fireworks, and when that sun hit the earth it turned into a strange three-legged crow. The air began to cool a little. Nine suns were left in the sky.

Like lightning one arrow after another flew from Yi's bow. The sky was filled with sparks and golden feathers; the earth grew cooler and cooler, and soon nine bewildered crows cawed on the ground.

All the while King Yao was watching. As the suns fell, he remembered how their old sun had warmed them after black night, how it ripened their harvest. So secretly he sent an official to steal away one of Yi's arrows. The frenzied archer reached back after his ninth arrow to grasp nothing but air, and pausing only then, he lowered his magnificent bow. Thus was Yi prevented from slaughtering all the suns, and he was praised by all the people.

The Tasks of Yi

Heroes famous for their strength often travel the world to test and hone their powers, helping people by vanquishing fearsome and evil forces. Yi was no exception. When he had rid King Yao of the nine suns, he set out adventuring over the earth. There are hundreds of tales recounting the monsters and pestilence that Yi battled. We present a selection here to show the variety of heroic tasks accomplished by Yi.

At that time on the central plain was a monster with a human face, horse's hoofs and a red oxlike body called Ya Yu. He was thought to be a small god from the heavens who had been murdered by Er Fu and Wei. Ya Yu could wail like a baby and terrified the people with his unearthly cries from the Ruoshui River, where he had turned into a monster. But brave Yi killed Ya Yu, and the people no longer trembled at his cries.

Next Yi turned south to fight the monster of the marsh, Zao Chi, which means "chisel teeth". Zao Chi was a creature with a human face, six feet and an animal head. At first the beast tried to fight valiant Yi with a spear, but when Yi took out his divine bow and arrow, the monster quickly raised his shield. Alas! Too late! The arrow pierced his heart and killed him.

Yi travelled north to Xiongshui River to look for another man-eating monster called Jiu Ying. This great nine-headed beast alternately breathed fire and water, and Yi waded into the turbulent water of the river to fight him. Exhausted and wounded, the beast finally sank into the depths, and a pool of red blood spread over the surface of the waters and disappeared.

It may have been around this time that the northern mountain Xilu suddenly collapsed. Yi was passing by when the mountain crumbled, and there he found in the rubble a solid jade finger guard which from that time he always carried with him to use when shooting his divine arrows.

In Qingqiu marsh to the east lived a vulture called Dafeng. The terrible bird was unnaturally strong, and Yi knew it could not be felled with his arrows. So he came up with a plan. He got a strong piece of cord and tied it to one end of the arrow. Then he hid himself in some bushes, and as the bird flew past, Yi raised his bow with a steady hand and true eye and shot Dafeng in the chest. Just as he thought, the bird was only wounded, but the arrow held fast. Yi had securely fastened the cord to a strong tree, and now he pulled down the flapping creature and slashed it dead with his sword.

At Dongting Lake in the south lived an enormous poisonous snake with a black body and green head called Ba Serpent. With a flick of its awful tail it could overturn a ship. It could swallow an elephant whole, disgorging the bones three years later. Ba Serpent was a fearful opponent.

On the shores the fishermen gathered to watch. Yi stepped into a light skiff and rowed to the middle of the lake. The snake, angered at this challenge to his supremacy, reared up out of the water, huge mouth agape, its firelike tongue flicking menacingly. Yi's arrows flew one after another like sparks from a whetting stone. The snake crumpled back, mortally wounded, but powerful rage coursed through its dying body and in its last throes it lunged at Yi's boat. The waves crashed, and with his sharp sword raised above his head, Yi slashed at the terrible monster. Again and again the snake reared up until the lake was thick with blood. Then finally Yi pierced it between the eyes and it sank heavily into the depths.

Local fishermen later dredged up the serpent's bones and piled them into a small hill, now called Baling Hill near Dongting Lake at the town of Yueyang.

Yi's last task was to kill a great boar in Sanglin Forest,

somewhere in the central plain. The beast ravaged the crops, bringing famine every year. Yi entered the deep forest to meet the fierce creature and skilfully shot arrows into its feet. As it lay flailing on the ground, Yi caught the boar alive. He tied it up, hauled it home, cooked it, and offered it to the Emperor of Heaven as a sacrifice. But the ways of gods are unpredictable and the god disdained Yi's gift. Perhaps he hated Yi for killing the suns. Who knows what will anger a god?

Thus was Yi banished to live as a mortal on earth. So he went home to the sighs of his wife, who had quickly tired of mortal life and yearned for the lightness of heaven. Complaints from his wife, indifference from the god, and not a friend to console brave Yi. He could bear his empty life no longer, and taking a cart and a quiver of arrows, he roamed for days at a time, crossing the wild plains and hunting deep in the forest.

Chang E Quests for Immortality

So Yi was exiled from the divine world, along with his wife, the fairy goddess Chang E.

It was Chang E who brooded darkly about their new mortal natures, Chang E who had so loved the magnificence of the gods' palace, the fine jade food, the dance of the phoenix. One day she said to her husband: "I don't really blame you for anything except that you were so hotheaded that you killed the god's nine suns. And you might have killed them all if you hadn't run out of arrows. Now we can never go back, and will go to the underworld when we die. It is horrible to think of living among all those black demons and ghosts after the Emperor's palace . . . Oh! What will become of us."

Yi had been out hunting and sat skinning his catch. He scarcely looked up—it was a refrain he had heard before. "Yes, I too do not relish the thought of death in the underworld, but my dear, what can I do?"

Now, Chang E had been thinking long and hard about her problem, and this was exactly the question she had hoped he would ask. She paused, as if thinking, then said, "Perhaps there is something you can do. I heard, you know, that there is a powerful god called Xi Wang Mu, who can control the life of mortals. He lives on Mount Kunlun."

"Hmm . . ."

"And he keeps the medicine of immortality."

Yi suddenly looked up and brightened to see his wife smiling warmly at him, the old sparkle in her eyes.

"You are right," he replied, smiling too. "Xi Wang Mu does indeed have such medicine. Tomorrow I will go and call on him."

So together they prepared a simple bag and food for the journey. At daybreak Yi was on his white horse, riding towards Mount Kunlun, his quiver over his shoulder, his bow slung across his back.

Mount Kunlun, the earthly palace of the Yellow Emperor, was encircled by burning mountains and a deep abyss. It was said that not even a feather could float on the Ruoshui River, much less a person in a boat. Although the people often spoke of the famous elixir of immortality kept safe by Xi Wang Mu, who could pass over the Ruoshui and through the burning mountains to the place where he lived?

Yi approached Mount Kunlun with his many powers. No one remembers how, but Yi the famous archer was able to cross the abyss; he penetrated the fiery mountains and scaled towering Mount Kunlun until he came to the rice that grew many feet high and saw the animal who guarded the Kaiming Gate. Before long he found the god.

Now Xi Wang Mu was a strange-looking god. He had a leopard's tail, tiger teeth and tangled hair which he covered with a painted jade hat. He could howl like a wolf, and besides guarding the secret of immortality he was a god of punishment and pestilence. In his cave he kept three red-headed, green-bodied birds who went out one by one in search of food for him.

Yi went directly to Xi Wang Mu and told him his story. He told how he'd killed the suns, how he'd been banished into mortality, of the sufferings of his beautiful wife. And Xi Wang Mu heard the story with an open heart. He reached into a secret place and brought out a small pouch of the medicine, enough for two people. Ceremoniously he handed it to Yi, saying:

"This medicine is made from the immortal fruit of Mount Kunlun's immortal trees. These trees bloom once every three thousand years and produce fruit once every six thousand years. There is little and here is all I have. If two people eat it, they will have immortality on earth, but if only one person eats it all, that person will become a divine immortal of the heaven. Now take it, and guard it carefully when you get home."

Yi retraced his path home, through the mountains of fire, over the deep abyss, across the plains and forest back to Chang E who awaited her husband impatiently. He recounted all his voyage and all that the god had told him. He warned her to take good care of the powerful medicine and placed the pouch in her outstretched hands.

"If one person takes it," he repeated, "that person will become a divine immortal. Keep it safe and we will find an auspicious day to eat it together."

Yi then returned to his hunting. As he wandered the woods he thought that without the threat of the underworld, life on this earth was good.

But Chang E sat at home nostalgically dreaming of her days as a goddess in heaven. She hid the little pouch, but each day she took it out and stared at it, remembering the beautiful flowers, the jade pastry and the music of the immortal world. And her thoughts circled round until they circled back to her husband.

"I suffer today because of him," she brooded. "I would be a goddess yet were it not for him. Oh, how I want to return to the heavens, to my rightful home!"

And with that thought she stared at the pouch and contemplated for the first time taking it all on her own. But she dared not . . . yet. She must seek a sign.

So Chang E hesitated and thought and hesitated again, and finally desire overcame her. She went to consult a witch called You Huang, and she asked the witch to divine her future.

You Huang took out of her a shell of a tortoise that was said to have lived one thousand years. The witch chanted softly. Her eyes half-closed and transfixed upon the powerful shell, she intoned these words:

Auspicious are the fortunes of this woman.
Clever, beautiful this woman.
Westward will she journey high above,

Far from wretched earth, high above.
Go, now go, no fear, no hesitation,
Go, now go, with prosperous expectation.

And hearing these words, Chang E leaned closer to the tortoise shell, a look of wonder passing over her face.

She hurried home, and one evening when Yi was out, she sat beside the open window, staring at the moon, thinking of the witch's words and fondling the little pouch. In the clear silver light she thought of home, the beautiful flowers and fruit, and hesitated no longer. She opened the bag of medicine and ate it all.

What changes in our fate are caused by a single gesture, a fleeting thought, a single swallow. Chang E felt herself becoming lighter and lighter. Oh, how lovely was her old state. She had almost forgotten. Lighter and lighter she grew, released from the heavy body of mortality, and she began to rise from the ground, passing through the open window up into the sky.

In the silent, moonlit night all was quiet and bright. She rose and rose until she was above a grey earth, the trees noiseless in the forests, even the beasts and insects still, unmoving. But in such tranquillity a terrible loneliness seared through Chang E.

"Why is everything so distant and still," she thought. "Why am I so alone and no one welcomes me?"

Even in her new lightness she began to brood: "How can I return to heaven? All those gods will scorn me for deserting my husband, all those goddesses will laugh at me in my solitude. But this earth is so grey and unwelcoming, what can I do?"

She floated there between two worlds. And the only light in the darkness was the moon. So, setting her determined mouth, she floated towards the moon. She would live there. On the moon there was no one to scorn her. But a terrible thing happened to her when she reached the moon. As she settled with a sigh to rest on its surface, she began to transform. Her back contorted stiffly, and her breasts spread flat and ugly, popping up in little bumps. Her mouth stretched wider and wider into a grotesque grin, and her eyes stretched into ugly round circles on both sides of her head. She had turned into a toad.

Poor Chang E, the beautiful goddess! She tried to croak out a cry for help, but there was no one to hear. She wanted to run away but could only leap and crouch, stuck for ever alone upon the moon.

Such was the earliest tale of the goddess Chang E.

But later stories end a little differently: Chang E did not change but only felt very lonely on the moon, where she found a rabbit and an old cassia tree. In these stories it is said a man called Wu Gang was exiled to the moon to cut the cassia tree as punishment for trying to become immortal. But the tree could never be cut. Each time the hatchet hit the trunk, the bark grew back again.

So it was that Chang E knew loneliness inside her, outside her, loneliness so heavy that all her wondrous lightness of being was forgotten. So it was that Chang E lived with a breaking heart, mourning her immortality, mourning her mortality, for ever on the moon.

And Yi? Yi came home from hunting with a fine catch that night and saw the empty pouch beside the open window. Now he was mortal. He sat alone all day watching the last sun of the sky fall into the western sea, watching the distant moon begin to rise.

Mi Fei, the Fairy

Fortune or misfortune, we cannot tell, lay in Yi's encounter with Mi Fei, fairy goddess of the Ruoshui River. Mi Fei (also called Ruobin) was the daughter of Tai Hou, god of the east, and drowned in the river once while crossing. She was renowned for her beauty; the romantic poet Qu Yuan (c. 340–278 BC) tells her story:

For the bright fairy Mi Fei
I ask Feng Long* to ride the clouds,
I ask Jian Xiu** to carry to her
My silk sash, my love words.
I wait as she hesitates.
Perhaps . . .
But she turns away.

---

*God of clouds.
**Messenger of Tai Hou.

In the night she goes back to Qiongshi,
In the morning she washes her hair.
Misty beauty in Yupan River
She wanders, no place to go.
Is she proud, indifferent?
Perhaps . . .
I give up and seek another.

When Yi first saw Mi Fei, she was on the riverbank near some other fairies on a warm autumn day. Some were gathering shining black genodermas, those magic mushrooms that hold the secret of longevity and can even bring the dead back to life. Others were gathering pearls and the feathers of coloured birds. Some were just strolling arm in arm along the river. Only little Mi Fei stood apart, gazing into the waters, silent and melancholy as the moon hanging in a dark sky dotted with wisps of cloud.

Her husband was He Bo, god of the river. Some say He Bo became god of the river when he drowned while crossing; others say he swallowed a magic medicinal herb and then entered the river and became immortal. He was very handsome and flirtatious with a powder-white face and a slender body. The lower part of his body was like a fish's. He Bo's favourite pastime was to ride in his water cart with its beautiful lotus-pod roof, drawn by his dragon. He wandered the rivers visiting all the fairies and nymphs. The poet Qu Yuan also described him:

Palace of pearls, purple shell gate,
Home of the river god in the deep.
He lounges on the white turtle,
With fairy maids he drifts all day.
The great river flows down to the sea.

Many folktales describe He Bo's dalliances and flirtations. Some say he married a human girl every year, others tell how much he loved such fine things as jade and pearls. He Bo had seen pretty Mi Fei and forced her to marry him, but she was soon cast aside by her wandering husband, left alone in her terrible solitude.

One day, standing apart from all the others on a cliff, Mi Fei saw Yi riding his white horse across the wild plain. Some say that

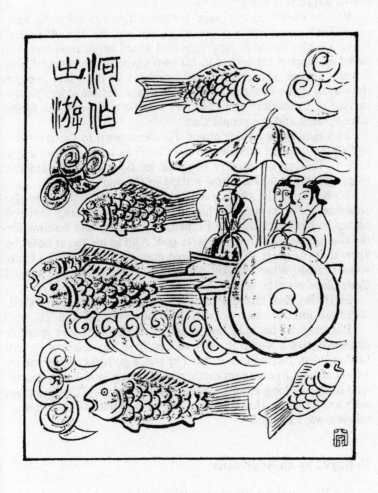

they saw in each other's eyes the pain of desertion. Who knows why it happens. They fell in love.

But He Bo would not stand for his wife's infidelity. He sent his officials and water nymphs to spy on her. He himself feared brave Yi, who had shot nine suns and killed seven monsters. He dared not oppose the archer in his own shape, so he changed into a white dragon who could swim concealed in the white caps of the waves. As he changed form, there was a terrible storm on the surface of the waters and the river overflowed. Soon the fields were flooded and the people fled.

This ignited Yi's quick anger. He went down to the riverside and stared into the turbulent waters until he could see the white dragon. Raising his mighty bow, he let fly his arrow into the swirling foam. And his arrow settled in the god's left eye.

With a howl the river god flew into the sky, straight to the Supreme Ruler, crying out his misfortune, demanding that the archer be punished. But the Emperor of Heaven had no time for the changeable, philandering river god. And in his secret heart he knew that the great Yi had suffered enough. He said: "Go back, white dragon. What are you doing on the surface of the waters! Your place is in the deep."

So He Bo, thus humiliated and rebuked by the Supreme God, dared not interfere any more in the love of Mi Fei and Yi.

But they did not stay long together. Sometimes love splashes gloriously like a waterfall only to end in a tiny shallow stream farther down the mountain. Mi Fei was a goddess of the waters who could not live long on earth, and Yi was a land-heavy mortal who could not long embrace her ethereal lightness. Their natures were too different. However deep, the love of mortals and immortals is always fleeting.

Betrayed by an Apprentice

As Yi wandered hunting in the forests and plains, he was accompanied by a follower called Feng Meng. And because Feng Meng proved himself intelligent and brave, Yi soon made him an apprentice.

To begin his training, Yi told Feng Meng, "To shoot well you

must first learn to look in the correct way. Go now and practise
gazing at an object without closing your eyes."

Feng Meng returned home to practise. He fixed his eyes on
his wife's loom. The shuttle slid back and forth, back and forth,
and he tried to stare unblinking. After practising for a long time,
he finally learned the skill. Even if someone thrust a finger
directly at his eye, he didn't blink.

Soon Feng Meng returned to Yi. This time Yi said, "Now for
the second step, you must learn to fix your eyes on a tiny object
and make that object grow very large."

Again Feng Meng returned home to practise. He tied a tiny
bug with an ox tail hair and hung it up. He stared and stared but
nothing happened. Finally after over a dozen days the bug seemed
to grow larger, expanding slowly in his eyes. Soon Feng Meng
could make a grain of dust as large as a wheel, an ordinary table
large as a hill.

When he reported to Yi his new skills, Yi was very pleased
with his student's accomplishment. "Now you may shoot with
me," he said, and as they spent their days together, he taught
almost all of his skills to Feng Meng.

After some time it seemed that Feng Meng could shoot as well
as Yi. Whenever people spoke of great archers, they always
mentioned in the same breath the names of Yi and Feng Meng,
and so both men were famous.

Once there was a shooting match between them. A row of
geese flew overhead, and Yi asked Feng Meng to shoot first.
Taking three arrows, Feng Meng raised his bow, and one, two,
three birds fell to the earth in but a moment, arrows accurately
through their heads. As these geese began falling, the other geese
in the sky scattered wildly in all directions. Yi then lifted his bow
and shot three arrows. Three geese fell to the earth, arrows
accurately through their heads, and Feng Meng recognized the
greater prowess of his teacher. Jealousy is the dark side of
admiration, especially jealousy of one's teacher. And the former
loyalty of Feng Meng soon turned into a jealous hatred towards
the man who had taught him everything.

Of course, at first Feng Meng remained respectful towards Yi.
But later, Yi grew moody as he brooded upon the injustice of the
gods towards him, over his unhappy loves, his loneliness. He

began to lose his temper frequently without great cause, cursing his attendants including Feng Meng for nothing. And Feng Meng, who no longer loved his master, began to find fault too. The spark of his jealousy now fanned into vengeful flames. Feng Meng decided to murder Yi and finally rid himself of this torment, his rival and his teacher.

One day Yi asked Feng Meng to go hunting, but the apprentice invented an excuse to stay at home, so Yi set off by himself. In the evening Yi returned on horseback along the road as was his custom. Suddenly he noticed a shadow moving behind a tree and saw an arrow flying towards him. Swiftly Yi grasped an arrow from his quiver and shot from the horse's back. The arrows met in the air, the two points cracking sharply against each other and falling to the ground. Another arrow flew from behind the tree, and again Yi shot and again the two arrows fell to the ground. Nine times the arrows flew, cracked, and fell, and then Yi's quiver was empty.

Feng Meng stepped out of the shadows, grimly, proudly lifting his last arrow to his bow. He drew back the taut bowstring and aimed at his master's throat.

Like lightning the arrow flew through the air, but Yi swiftly dropped his head. The arrow hit his mouth; he fell backwards from his mount to the ground. Feng Meng stepped forward to look down on the dead man's face.

But just as he was bending in triumph over the man, Yi opened his eyes! He sat straight up and whipped the arrow from his mouth. In a flash he lifted it to his bow and shot at his apprentice's face.

Feng Meng uttered a sharp cry, and holding his head in his hands, turned and ran. The arrow followed. Feng Meng tried to duck behind the tree, but to his horror, the arrow turned and still followed. He darted back and forth, circling the tree, and as if the arrow had eyes, it followed him everywhere. When Feng Meng tired and slowed, the arrow too slowed down; when Feng Meng made a quick dash, the arrow kept pace.

Breathless, glowing with sweat, Feng Meng cried, "Master . . . master, forgive me!"

Yi waved his hand and spat out in disgust, "Away with you!" Suddenly the arrow dropped to the ground.

Feng Meng stopped then, wiping the sweat from his face. He slowly approached the master, face turned away in shame.

"Foolish!" growled Yi, "After studying with me for such a long time!" Slowly then he smiled, "You have not learned the skill of 'biting' arrows. Learn from this mistake."

Feng Meng only mumbled, his head low, "Yes . . . master."

The wise teacher is the one who responds with benevolence to the student's errors. Yi was master of his skills and knew himself. For some time after, Feng Meng showed a humble face to the master archer, and again they began to hunt together. Yi wished to believe that his student had learned a lesson.

But Feng Meng's heart, now humiliated, was still full of hatred. He carved himself a heavy peach-wood stick and carried it with him hunting, using it to beat wild animals and carry them. Yi, trusting, was unaware of his danger.

One day, together, they went to the edge of a lake to shoot geese. Yi was aiming up at the sky while the apprentice busied himself at his back. Just as Yi lifted his bow for a second shot, Feng Meng crept up behind him, lifted the stick and brought it down hard over the master's head. Yi had sensed something and was just beginning to turn around when the stick crashed into his skull, and blood gushed from his ears.

The master archer's bow fell to the ground. With his last breath of strength Yi looked with a dreadful sneer towards the younger man, then he crumpled to the waiting earth.

Thus the tragic death of Yi. It is said that later the people worshipped him as the god called Zongbu, in remembrance of his work to rid the earth of pestilence. But only in death did Yi know honour, for in life all those who had been closest to Yi had turned their backs on him.

Gun Battles the Great Flood

During the reign of Yao there was a great disaster, a terrible flood which lasted twenty-two years into the reign of Shun. Some history books say that Gun tried to contain the flood with dikes; and when the waters overflowed, wreaking more destruction, he was executed on Mount Yushan.

The version we present here is based on Qu Yuan's writings, in which Gun is a good man who almost succeeds in tricking the Emperor of Heaven. After he is killed, his son Yu inherits his spirit and heroically conquers the flood for his father.

During the reign of Yao there came a terrible flood.

The whole earth was submerged, and all the world was an endless ocean. People floated on the treacherous waters, searching out caves and trees on high mountains. The crops were ruined, and survivors vied with fierce birds and beasts for places to live. Thousands drowned each day; and looking over the floating corpses, King Yao felt a knife pierce his heart.

He called together his dukes and officials and said: "The flood rises every day. The hills and mountains grow smaller and smaller. Our subjects who are not drowned are being killed by the wild animals. Who among us can lead the people out of this terrible disaster?"

And after consultation, those dukes and officials said: "Let the great Gun try."

The records say that Gun was a white horse, son of Luo Ming and grandson of the Yellow Emperor himself; but upon hearing this advice, Yao shook his head. Heavy with the weight of disaster he answered: "I know Gun. He is a brave man, but not so wise." But the dukes and officials insisted that there was no one else, and so Gun was asked to attempt the task. However, it was Gun himself who had expressed his desire to help; only Gun among the many gods and goddesses in the divine palace felt sympathy for the plight of the people. He was angered by the Yellow Emperor's neglect of the world, but the Supreme God refused to help and was unmoved by his grandson's pleas.

So Gun decided to descend to earth himself and conquer the flood. He sat devising strategies, perplexed by the Supreme God's invincible power, when he noticed an eagle and a tortoise hobbling towards him, each helping the other.

"Gun," they said, "Why are you looking so sad?"

And Gun told them he wanted to get rid of the flood but didn't know how.

"But it is not so difficult to get rid of the flood." They said together.

Gun looked up wth interest. "How?"

And so the eagle and the tortoise told Gun about the substance called Xi Rang, Endless Earth. It looked like a small clod of earth, but when dropped in the world it could grow into mountains or dams. Gun was very pleased.

"But where can I get this Endless Earth?"

The eagle and tortoise lowered their voices, "It is the most treasured possession of the Supreme God."

We do not know where this divine possession was kept hidden or the story of how Gun got it. We only know that he did, and that he flew away from the divine palace hiding the gift.

All watched with wonder as he placed the Endless Earth into the muddy waters. Mountains and dams sprang up; the earth drank in those flood waters. Soon land reappeared everywhere and the waters fell back into the oceans. Thin, dark-faced people crawled down from the trees and out of the shadowy caves. They honoured Gun and hailed him as their hero, and began once more to build homes and towns.

But the disaster was not yet abated. The Supreme God learned of his own grandson's theft and flew into a rage. He ordered his official Zhu Rong down to the earth.

"Seize back my Endless Earth, and kill that scoundrel Gun!"

Away hurried the fire god with the divine edict. On Mount Yushan he found Gun and murdered him. Then he stole back the Supreme God's earth. In crashed the great flood waters once more, and even as they sorrowed for Gun's death, the people had to fight again for their lives.

Mount Yushan is said to have been at the end of the north—a dark and desolate place without sunlight. There brave Gun sacrificed his life to help save Yao's people. He regretted not his own death nor his own thwarted heroism. But he mourned that he had failed and that those people still suffered. How could he lie at peace in this dark place?

And so the spirit of Gun would not leave him. His body did not decompose for three years; and strangest of all, a new life, a son who would be called Yu, was growing inside his belly, nourished by the divine qualities he was inheriting from his father, Gun.

When the strange news came to the attention of the Supreme

God, he feared that Gun would become an evil spirit and plague him, so he ordered one of his officials to go and cut open the belly of the strange corpse. The official flew down to Mount Yushan carrying in his belt a divine knife called the *Wudao*.

But a strange thing happened. As the official slit open Gun's belly, a fabulous dragon with a pair of sharp horns burst up and coiled high into the sky. This was Yu, Gun's son. And Gun too transformed into a yellow dragon, flying away to the Yuyuan Abyss at the foot of Mount Yushan.

It is said that the yellow dragon who had once been Gun has little power. All his strength was given to Yu, his son, the one who would complete his father's task.

Yu Conquers the Flood

Yu is now generally considered to be the first king of the Xia Dynasty (21–16 BC) and was probably an actual person who has turned into a legendary hero. His main work was to control the flood, which he did for thirteen years. One of the first written accounts of Yu is in *Records of the Historian*. That version emphasizes Yu's devotion to duty, as when he ignores the cries of his own son in order to complete his work. Yu represents the qualities of intelligence, strong leadership directed towards the task at hand, and devotion to duty that are intrinsic to the Chinese understanding of the hero.

The Defeat of Gong Gong

The golden dragon flew through the sky, heralding an end to suffering. Even the Supreme God himself was a little surprised at this mysterious creature who sprang from the body of dead Gun, and he thought to himself, "The rebelling spirit of the father has been passed to the son and may even pass through the generations. Perhaps the people have suffered long enough."

And thus it was that the Yellow Emperor decided to yield to Yu, son of Gun. First he gave him the Endless Earth with instructions to use it to end the flood and relieve the people's suffering. Then he asked the dragon Ying Long (who had accomplished many heroic deeds in the wars with Chi You) to help Yu in his task.

So Yu received all the things to fight the flood. With Ying Long and his dragon followers they all decided how to regulate the rivers.

Yet even such help from the Supreme God could not ensure success, for Gong Gong had been angered. Gong Gong, god of the waters, had long before been ordered to create the flood, and he was not willing so soon to abandon his power to that upstart boy-dragon.

Yu saw that Gong Gong would not be reasoned with. He decided to follow his great-grandfather's example, and he called together all the spirits and fairies of the earth. To Mount Huiji they all came, all except the one called Fang Feng Shi, who arrived late. Yu flew into a rage at Fang Feng Shi's negligence and ordered him immediately executed. All watched with awe and shock, and from that time no one dared disobey the mysterious dragon's commands. (In the writings of Confucius we have a note about the skeleton of Fang Feng Shi. It is said that during the Spring and Autumn Period, the Wu state attacked the State of Yue, surrounding King Gou Jian's residence in Mount Huiji. During the ferocious fighting the whole mountain was destroyed, and there they found an enormous strange skeleton. Some people then went to ask Confucius, a man of profound learning, and he told how Fang Feng Shi was killed in a battle with Yu.)

Once Yu had finished with the god of the waters, he was able to tackle the flood. First he ordered an enormous turtle to follow him carrying the Endless Earth. He heard the cries of drowning people and rushed to them, dropping little clods of the magic substance. As it sprang into mountains and spread into land, the people began to crawl up and stand once more upon solid ground. Yu knew it was not enough to simply create earth again; he knew that he must also regulate the course of the rivers so that the flood water would flow down towards the sea. He led all the fairies and spirits in this task. He ordered the dragon Ying Long to proceed first, dragging his tail, scoring the earth with deep scratches. Then the fairies and spirits dug shallow gullies along the marks and the water began to flow seaward, creating the rivers of China today.

Regulation of the Rivers

How was it that Yu knew where to direct the great Yellow River? Some say that he was standing on a high cliff overlooking the flood when he noticed a spirit floating on the surface of the waves, a spirit with a white human face and the long body of a fish. This creature handed Yu a wet flat rock scored by a number of marks. Staring at it, Yu understood that these marks were a map of the course of the rivers, and he used it as his guide. Some say that this helpful spirit was He Bo, god of the rivers.

There are also stories that describe how when Yu was opening a tunnel at Longmen (Dragon Gate) Mountain, he was helped by another deity. He had entered a long, dark cave and could see almost nothing in the darkness. He lit a torch to continue on his way and suddenly noticed a flash of light and a black horned snake. The light was a shining white pearl glowing luminous from the snake's mouth. Yu extinguished his torch and followed the snake until he came to the bright opening of what seemed like a palace, where people in black flanked a god with a human face and a snake's body.

"Are you not Fu Xi, son of Hua Xu Shi, fairy of the nine rivers?" asked brave Yu.

"I am," the god replied gravely.

Together they talked, for Fu Xi had suffered in the flood and he greatly admired Yu's work. He offered Yu a jade ruler, about twelve inches long, which would help in his measurements and regulation of the rivers.

Dragon Gate Mountain was originally in the chain of Luliang Mountains along the border of today's Shanxi and Shaanxi provinces. But it stood in the way of the course of the Yellow River. So when Yu came to the mountain and the water began flowing upwards, with a lash from his divine hand he split the mountain into two parts, west and east. There the rushing water poured down over the steep cliffs as if they were a gate. The fish gather there each late spring to hold a jumping competition, and those who can jump over the gate become dragons and fly away into

the sky. Near Dragon Gate there is also a place called Carp
Valley, where the carp gather each spring trying to jump the falls.

About three hundred *li* downstream from Dragon Gate is a
gorge with three smaller gates called Sanmen (Three Gates)
Gorge. Certain legends say that Yu had chopped the enormous
mountain into three parts. Each gate has its own name: Gate of
Ghosts, Gate of Fairies, Gate of People. And by the Three Gates
Gorge, there are still seven stone wells left by Yu as he led the
regulation of the rivers.

Today you will see that the river flows eastward into the
narrow gorge. Two rocky hills stand upright in the middle of the
gorge, so the waters rush over the hills in three great rapids.

Help from the Fairy Yao Ji

The regulation of the rivers was fraught with dangers and
setbacks. One year Yu and his people were working in Ba Zhu at
the foot of Wushan Mountain (now in Sichuan Province). They
were cutting trees and digging the earth when a sudden violent
storm blew up. Black clouds darkened the sky, rocks flew through
the air on heavy winds, the very cliffs and mountains trembled.
Rough waves blew up like hills, and Yu's people scattered out of
the way of disaster like autumn leaves. Powerful as he was, Yu
could not control the storm.

Suddenly the goddess Yao Ji appeared in the place. Some said
she was one of the Fiery Emperor's daughters; others said she was
the daughter of Xi Wang Mu. She cultivated her fairy powers
while still a child until she could change her shape at will and
became a powerful goddess in the heavens.

That autumn Yao Ji was travelling on floating clouds over the
eastern sea, enjoying the scenery of Wushan Mountain. As she
descended from the clouds, she noticed the river directed by Yu;
and when she learned of Yu's struggle, she flew to where he was
working.

Yu knew of Yao Ji's reputation and asked her help against the
storms and thunders. So Yao Ji assigned a fairy maidservant to
Yu to teach him magic arts, which he quickly mastered.

Then Yao Ji sent Yu more servants to help him: Kuang

Zhang, Yu Yu, Huang Mo, Da Yi and Geng Chen. They grasped the thunder and lightning and used them to bore a tunnel right through Wushan Mountain where the flood waters could drain. And so were the people saved.

Yu then went to thank the goddess for her help. He thought he saw her standing on a cliff of the mountain where she had first descended from the clouds, but as he approached the place, he saw only a huge rock growing larger and larger. When he came a few steps closer, the stone began to change shape, then rose and turned into a wispy cloud. The cloud floated through the air and became a magnificent white crane wheeling through the sky. Suddenly it turned into a dragon whirling larger and larger, surrounded and finally hidden by thick, dark grey clouds. And then on Yu's amazed, upturned face fell soft drops of fresh rain . . .

Yu was curious about the goddess. Why did she make herself so changeable, so mysterious? He went to ask her servant, Tong Lu. But Tong Lu only smiled and said: "She is not strange, but the daughter of a powerful god. It is because she knows the secret of transformation that she was able to help you."

Yu said: "But how can I thank her?"

Tong Lu then pointed to the sky and Yu looked up. There floating in the mountains was a richly decorated jade palace guarded by two lions at the gate. Fierce dragons and strange beasts stood along both sides of the road, a heavenly steed leading the way. At the end, Yao Ji herself sat gentle and grave on a precious jade throne, her maidservants gathered about her.

Without knowing how he got there, Yu suddenly found himself walking into the palace. He knelt with a low bow and thanked Yao Ji for her help. Before the goddess had finished modestly declining thanks, Yu eagerly asked her if she knew other means of controlling the flood. Thereupon the fairy ordered Lin Yonghua to bring out a red jade box. Inside the box was a heavenly scroll. Solemnly she handed it to Yu, telling him that with this knowledge and her two followers Geng Chen and Yu Yu, he could accomplish his task.

It is said that this goddess was deeply attached to the people and the beauty of Wushan Mountain. Each day from a cliff she watched the gorges plunging hundred *li* down into the river. Many ships were lost in the treacherous torrents. So the goddess sent hundreds of divine birds to fly over the gorge and guide the boats. And as Yao Ji stood there, year after year, it is said that she changed into many mountains, which in her honour the people call "Goddess Peaks".

But the struggle against the flood was long.

At one time a weary dragon grew careless and lost his way. He scratched the earth, and the fairies dug and laboured over a useless valley. Not until many *li* were completed did Yu learn of the mistake. Furious at the waste of his precious labour, Yu tossed the foolish dragon to his death from the top of a cliff. Today in Wushan County we can still see the Cuokai (wrongly opened) Valley and stand on the Dragon Execution Terrace.

Another time Yu was working at the Tongbo Mountains and was forced by strong winds and thunder to turn back many times. He soon learned there was a terrible water monster, Wu Zhi Qi, between the Huaishui and Woshui rivers. This monster looked like a monkey with a high forehead, low flattened nose, white face and green body. Its teeth and eyes glittered, and it had the strength of nine elephants and could stretch its head out over a hundred feet. The Wu Zhi Qi monster moved so swiftly, jumping and writhing, that no one had ever captured it.

Even Yu's powers were worthless against the creature. He asked Tong Lu and Wu Muyou to subdue it. But they couldn't, and eventually it was Geng Chen who fought the monster. While they struggled, thousands of water nymphs and mountain spirits appeared in defence of the creature, but Geng Chen raised a great spear and pierced the monster, subduing it until Yu had time to snap an iron chain around its neck. Then they put a chain with a golden bell through its nose and tied it to Guishan Mountain, which is now in Huaiyin County, Jiangsu Province.

The Marriage of Yu

Once passing Mount Tushan (now in Shaoxing, Zhejiang Province), Yu thought, "I am thirty years old. It is now time to marry!" And at that very moment he saw a nine-tailed fox approaching him, which reminded him of a local folk song:

> *He who meets the fox with nine tails*
> *Will become king of the land.*
> *He who marries the chief's daughter of Mount Tushan*
> *Will become a prosperous man.*

This chief's daughter was Nu Jiao, reputed for her beauty and grace. But Yu had so much river work to do that he was reluctant to offer the girl a proposal and so he left for the south. The people told Nu Jiao of Yu's desire for her. He was a distant hero and the girl began to love him. She sent her maidservants each day for news of Yu's return, and while the gentle girl awaited her hero she composed this song:

> *Waiting for you*
> *Time seems so long.*

This simple poem is said to be the earliest southern song.

When Yu finally returned from the south he intended to propose to Nu Jiao, and to his surprise he found maidservants waiting for him with a message of love from their mistress. So it was that the two finally met and married at a place called Taisang.

Only four days after the wedding Yu left Nu Jiao to continue his work. He sent her to live in Anyi (in today's Shanxi Province), and when he heard that she was homesick he ordered his men to build her a high tower. From the top, she could gaze across the land towards her hometown many thousand *li* away.

But poor Nu Jiao's solitude was too deep to bear, with neither her hometown nor her husband to comfort her. So she decided to follow Yu and help however she could.

Now at that time they were working in the treacherous Huan-yuan Mountains (in southwest Yanshi County, Henan Province). The mountain was steep, and they had to skirt enormous boulders to reach its summit. Yu said to his wife, "The task today is difficult and you must stay away. I will hang a drum over the cliff, and when you hear it you may then come to me."

As soon as Nu Jiao left, Yu turned into a strong black bear, digging a pit into the mountain with mighty claws. He tossed boulder after boulder out behind him, and it just happened that some flying stones hit upon the drum.

Of course Nu Jiao heard the echo and hurried up the

mountain with food for her husband. She was frightened to see the horrible bear, and uttering a cry she dropped her basket and turned to run away. Not realizing that he had forgotten to change back into his human shape, Yu began to follow her. All that Nu Jiao saw was a ferocious bear running after her, and she grew more terrified. Faster and faster they ran until they reached the foot of Songgao Mountain (today's Mount Songshan in Henan Province), the poor girl's muscles growing stiffer and stiffer. Petrified, she turned into a rock, and Yu, frightened and angry, called out to her: "My son! Leave to me my son!"

Then the north side of the rock cracked open and a baby tumbled out of the side. Strange things happened during those years of regulating the rivers, and the birth of Yu's child from a rock was as strange as Yu's own birth from a corpse. Yu picked up the child and said: "I will call you Qi (cracked open), and when you are grown up, you too will help battle the rivers."

Where Yu Travelled While Controlling the Flood

Yu travelled all over the world, to a hundred different states, while doing his work. He was in Fusang, the place where the sun rose, and travelled through Jiujing to the plains of Qingqiang, brightly lit under the sun. He passed by Cuanshu, where a thousand trees covered the land like clouds, and he climbed to the summit of Mentian (touch the heavens) Mountain. He made his way across the State of Heichi (black teeth), so called because the people there have black teeth, and the country called Niaogu, which means "birds valley". In Qingqiu he saw the nine-tailed foxes, and later he proceeded southward through the tropical growth into the State of Jiaozhi, which is now called Vietnam.

Yu travelled far and wide. The fragments record his visits to Sunpo, Xuman, Dansu, Qishu, and Feishuipiaopiao states. He climbed the Jiuyang Mountains, lived for a while in Yumin State, where the people all had wings, and also in the State of

Luomin, where the people wore no clothes, as well as in Busi State, where people didn't die.

When he turned westward he came to the Sanwei Mountains, where Xi Wang Mu and his three birds lived. At Jijin (gold pile) Mountain he saw heaps of gold. He crossed the State of Qigong, where people have only one hand and one foot, and found another place where people have one hand and three faces. It is also said that Yu visited forgotten fairy realms where the people lived on dew and air.

Yu travelled far and wide. Stories record his visits to northern places, unknown to us: Renzheng, Quanrong, Kuafu, Jishui, and Jishi, onward also to Xiahai and Hengshan. Some say they must have been at the farthest ends of the north because he met Yu Qiang, the great north sea god of the wind and waters.

Once Yu saw a long, bleak mountain range, where there was no sign of life. He climbed over the peaks and saw on the other side a strange, bare plain where only a few streams crossed the landscape like cobwebs. But there, beside the streams, were men and women, young and old, dancing, strolling and sleeping. Yu saw an old man cupping his hands to drink from one of the streams, but when he straightened up to leave, he felt himself stumbling as if drunk. Then he lay down and slept deeply, the others in this strange place paying him no heed at all.

Curious, Yu left and when reaching the foot of the mountain he found that he was in the State of Zhongbei (Northern Border), a place located in a protected valley of a long mountain range. From the top of Huling Hill, which looked like a vase, flowed a stream in all directions over the state. It was an extraordinary water called Shenfen; it tasted sweet, and a sip of it could appease all hunger and thirst. But too much made people so drunk they would sleep for ten days. In this place the weather was always pleasant, neither hot nor cold, without winds or rain or frost or snow. It was a place of eternal spring. For a while Yu stayed in this place, and the life of the people there was lovely indeed, for they never needed worry about food or clothing, tilling or weaving. Happily they drank the Shenfen water, danced and slept, and when they had lived a hundred years they lay down on the earth and died.

The Nine-headed Monster

Even after Yu subdued and regulated the rivers, he fought one last battle against the cruel Xiang Liu, a nine-headed monster who was an official of Gong Gong's. His nine terrible heads could eat on nine different mountains at the same time, and worse still, whatever the monster touched turned into poisonous marsh. People would die if they drank the brackish water, and even the animals could not survive it.

When Yu heard of this dangerous creature, he went and killed it; he slashed and stabbed, and stinking blood poured out of the nine heads, polluting the land and water. Three times Yu tried to make a dam to stop up the foul slime, and three times the earth gave way. Finally Yu dug a deep pool to hold the reeking blood. Later the four heavenly emperors built a terrace on the north side of Mount Kunlun overlooking this pool to remember the spot.

Now Yu finally felt that he had fulfilled the will of his father. He bade two divine officials, Da Zhang and Shu Hai, to measure the land. One measured from east to west, the other from north to south. Both officials arrived at the same measurement: two hundred million, thirty-three thousand, five hundred and seventy-five feet long. In Yu's time, it appears, this land was in the shape of a square. They counted also two hundred million, thirty-three thousand, five hundred and seventy-five abysses which were hundreds of feet deep. Many of these abysses were filled by Yu, but the magic power of that Endless Earth sometimes overflowed to create the mountains of China today.

So this was the new world created from the vision of Yu and his father Gun. The ruler Shun (heir of King Yao) offered Yu control of the kingdom, impressed by his dedication and tenacity. Some records say King Shun presented Yu with a piece of black jade, of which the upper part was square and the lower round. Other records say that the black jade was presented by a messenger from the Supreme God himself. This messenger was a long-bodied, long-tailed, human-shaped creature named Zhang Cheng. Because he sprang from the spirit of the Nine Virtues, he had the privilege of presenting this jade to Yu.

Yu's labours won him many honours. A divine horse named Fei Tu came and offered himself into Yu's service. Another animal called Jueti was said to have come from Hou Tu, god of the underworld. Both these horses could cover three thousand *li* in a single day. Some legends say that the Supreme God even offered Yu a beautiful fairy wife named Sheng Gu. And at the foot of Mount Huiji is a temple for Yu, housing a statue of his fairy wife.

Legendary Vessels

After Yu became king, he had nine enormous vessels cast of the best iron and bronze in the country. The art of these pieces was famous well into the later dynasties. Some say they were so heavy that they could be moved only by ninety thousand people. Myriad poisonous creatures, interwoven with devils and ghosts, nymphs and monsters, were engraved round the sides in bronze. The vessels were displayed in front of Yu's palace to teach the people about the creatures they might meet when they entered the forests. They served as an ancient travel guide, recounting all that Yu had learned in his years of wandering and regulating the waters.

These vessels were exhibited during the Xia, Yin, and Zhou dynasties. Later they were hidden in imperial temples by various kings and were the source of many conflicts. Every ambitious leader wanted to own them. During the Warring States Period, King Zhuang of Chu led his troops to attack Luhun. As they were passing by the capital making ready for battle, King Ding of Zhou sent his special envoy Wang Sunman to invite the travelling king to a banquet. At the end of the banquet the king pretended to be very drunk and asked Wang Sunman what these precious vessels weighed. But the witty Wang Sunman replied ironically, "Their weight lies in their excellence."

Embarrassed, the ambitious king then led his troops back to his own state.

At the end of the Spring and Autumn Period, Zhao Xiang,

the king of the Qin State, attacked Western Zhou and pillaged
these nine precious vessels. There is a curious story about their
transport back. It is said that one of them suddenly flew up
into the sky and fell back into the Sishui River. With an
enormous splash, the vessel sank and disappeared. The king was
disappointed to receive only eight, but there was nothing to be
done. Many years later his great-grandson, the First Emperor
of Qin, conquered the six states, unified China, and went
searching in vain for the immortals. As he was returning home
through a place called Pengcheng, he remembered having heard
recounted as a boy the story of the Sishui River's ninth vessel.
He ordered thousands of men to participate in dredging the
river for it. He never found it, and mysteriously the other eight
vessels also disappeared.*

The Death of Yu

Yu was long held in honour by his people. He had conquered
the flood and regulated the rivers. More than thirteen years had
he laboured, traversing the entire land. His hands and feet were
callus-covered, his nails and body hair were worn away. They say
that he never paused, even when he passed by his city and heard
the wails of his own small son. He limped from muscles withered
in the freezing winter waters. His skin was black from the winds
and the summer sun.

No one knows what happened to Yu. Some say he was buried
in Mount Huiji, where he had first called together all the nymphs
and spirits and fairies, the place where he married Nu Jiao. But
others think that even if his body was left on earth, Yu really
ascended to heaven, where he rested as a god. No one really
knows. But there is a tomb said to be Yu's cave, and the birds go
there each year to tend and honour Yu's tomb.

---

*In Wuliang Temple (Jiaxiang, Shandong Province) a Han Dynasty
fresco depicts the men of the First Emperor of Qin dredging the river from
a great bridge. The vessel is tied with ropes and has been dragged to the
surface, but there is an enormous dragon's head appearing out of the cast
metal, breaking the ropes with its teeth.

Ten Thousand Strange Sights, Ten Thousand Strange Creatures: *Shanhaijing*

At the end of the flood, we move from the ancient legendary heroes to the early kings of state. But in those legendary times there was another whole realm of creation. Books such as *Shanhaijing* (*Book of Mountains and Seas*) provide a kind of first encyclopaedia of all the monsters and fairies and strange things that ancient peoples encountered on earth. No story of Chinese mythology is complete without them, yet they make strange reading to our modern eyes. Like such fragmented texts from early western civilization as the broken tablets of the Gilgamesh epic, we hear only bits and pieces of the story and must trust our own imaginations to fill in the gaps. The simplicity of the language of the *Book of Mountains and Seas*, the directness of its descriptions of bizarre creatures and lost mountains, attest to a perception of the world in which the distinctions between dream, imagination, hearsay, nature, and objective reality were fluid and different from our own. We sense the primordial desire to have knowledge and power through naming. The records are full of lists of place names and names of forgotten creatures, of lineages and classifications. As an example of this voice speaking to us from fragments over 2,500 years old, listen to the opening lines of the *Book of Mountains and Seas*:

In front of Nanshanjin is called Queshan
And in front of Suishan is called Zhouyaoshan.
And beside the West Sea
are many Gui trees
and metals and jade
and much grass that looks like wheat
but shines translucent green.
Its name is Zhouyou,
Eat it and you are never hungry.
And beside the West Sea
are many trees that look like rice stalks
but they are black inside
and shine to the four directions.
Their name is Migu,
Wear them and you are never lost.
A beast is there like the monkey
but with white ears
and crawling on all fours
it can run like a man.

Its name is Shengsheng,
Eat it and you are a good runner.
The Limei River begins here
and flows west into the sea.

The following selection of fragments from *Shanhaijing* has been arranged to read more continuously than the difficult original. The fragments are presented with some old engravings of the ancient creatures which were so feared, so fascinating, that they were given the gift of a name and shaped into the human story.

The South

There is a place deep in the southwest called Jiexiong State. The people are winged with protruding foreheads and chests. Living there are birds called Biyi who are like wild ducks with green and red feathers but only one eye, one wing and one leg. They always fly in pairs. So Biyi (which means "wing to wing") is a symbol of the love between a man and a woman devoted to each other. These birds are also called Jiaojian, and whoever rides on their backs can live ten thousand years.

In the southeast is the State of Yumin (which means "winged people"). The people here have a long head with white hair, red eyes and a little beak. They have two small wings on their backs and can fly over a short distance. A kind of phoenix, the *luan* bird, lives here too. People eat the *luan* bird eggs and live like fairies.

Further southeast is another state called Huantou or sometimes Huanzhu. The people here are also birdlike, but they use their wings for walking sticks and catch shrimp and fish along the seashore with their sharp beaks. These people are thought to be the descendants of the family of Yao. They come from a man who committed suicide in the South Sea when he was found guilty of a crime. But Yao had pity on him and sent his sons to make sacrifices, so the man became a small birdlike creature.

In Yahuo State the people are black and look like monkeys. They eat burning charcoal and carry the glowing ember from place to place.

A little to the east is Sanmiao, where the descendants of the

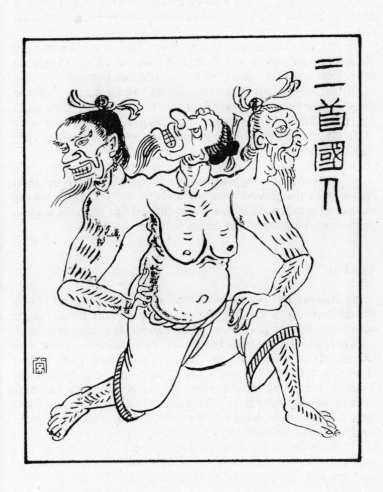

three Miao tribes live. When King Yao offered his kingship to Shun, they fought against Yao led by his son Dan Zhu. They live on the South Sea and have a small pair of wings under both their arms.

In Zhi State the people descend from Wuyin, the son of King Shun. They are yellow and skilled at snake shooting. They have much food and it is a peaceful and prosperous place.

To the east is the State of Jiaojing, which means "crossed shins". These people are only four feet tall; and since their shins are crossed, they cannot stand up unless someone helps them.

In the State of Fanshe are people with reversed tongues. They speak a language no one understands.

And in the State of Sanshou, people have three heads.

In the State of Changbi are people with arms so long that their hands touch the ground even when they are standing. Some say their arms are three *zhang* long, and they like to go to the sea and reach down with their bare hands to catch the fish.

The East

In Heichi State people have teeth dark as black paint. These are descendants of Di Jun and they live not far from Tanggu where the ten suns once were. They like to eat snakes and rice.

There are people who are black from the waist down who live near the sea in Xuangu State. They make their clothes from fish skins, and seagulls are their food. Near by live the Yushiqie tribe, who are also black. Sometimes they hold a snake in both hands; sometimes they hold a turtle in one hand and have a green snake hanging from the left ear and a red snake hanging from the right.

In the State of Maomin are hairy people. Their hair is very wiry and they live in mountain caves, never wearing clothes all year round.

The North

In the place called Qizhong or Fanzhong (reversed soles) the

people's feet face the wrong direction. Some say they only walk on their toes, but others say it looks always as if they're walking backwards.

In the State of Juying are people with great lumps upon their necks. They have to hold them when they walk to relieve the weight. The *xun* tree that grows a thousand *li* tall is found here too.

In the State of Nie'er or Daner are people with ears so heavy they have to hold them with both their hands. When they sleep, they use one ear as a mat and the other as a covering. These people each keep two big tigers for their servants.

In the place called Wuchang or Wufu, the people have no intestines. When they eat, the food goes straight down and is excreted with no digestion.

The people of Shenmu State have deep eye sockets and like to eat fish.

The descendants of Nie'er live in the State of Rouli, sometimes called Niuli or Liuli. These people have no bones and only one hand and foot, which are soft as a piece of flesh.

The descendants of Shao Hao are all called Wei. Having only one eye in the centre of their foreheads, they live in the State of One Eye.

The West

In the State of Changgu everyone has long legs, some say three *zhang* long.

In the State of Sushen the cave people wear pigskin clothes. During winter they paint themselves with thick animal grease. Sometimes they wear the bark of the *luotang* tree. They are skilled hunters and their bows are four feet long.

The Baimin State is the home of the descendants of Di Shun. They have white skin and white hair. In Baimin live beasts called Shenghuang which look like foxes with two horns on their heads. Sometimes they are called Feihuang because they run so fast they seem to fly. Whoever rides on them will live two thousand years.

In the State of Wuomin are phoenixes and *luan* birds and

much fertile land. Here the people eat plenty of eggs and drink fresh dew from the sky.

In the State of Xuanyuan people live a long time. The youngest die after eight hundred years. Since the Yellow Emperor has the name Xuanyuan, some think those people are his descendants. They all have human heads with snake's bodies and tails curving up around their necks. In the west also is a hill called Xuanyuan guarded by four snakes. No one can shoot arrows at this hill.

In the State of Women there are no men. The girls grow up and bathe in the pool called Huangchi, where they can get pregnant. If a baby is male, it dies before the age of three because here only girl-children survive.

Witches live in the State of Wuxian. Most famous among them are Wuxian, Wuji, Wufen, Wupeng, Wugu, Wuzhen, Wuli, Wudi, Wuxie and Wuluo. They travel from Mount Dengbao to the sky, taking messages between the heavens and earth. They like to carry a green snake in the left hand and a red snake in the right. And in that state are strange piglike animals called Bingfeng. They have a head at each end of their body.

In the State of Men there are no women. The men here are very gentle and can bear two sons each. Their babies come out between their ribs, and their bodies are made of shadows.

There is the One-armed State where people have only one arm, one eye and one nostril. The horses here too have only one leg and one eye and are striped yellow like a tiger.

The wife of Di Jun gave birth to the ancestors of Sanshen State. They all have one head and three bodies.

Clever people live in the State of Qigu. Some say they have one hand and three eyes, others say that they have one leg. They make special hunting traps and flying carts. Some say they once flew to Yuzhou during the Yin Dynasty. But these carts were feared and destroyed. They like to ride on strange, red and white spotted bird-horses who have two heads and coloured feathers. Whoever rides on them can live a thousand years.

So these are the strange places and creatures. This is how the world used to be.

Chapter 5
THREE DYNASTIES

The stories of the rise and fall of the first three dynasties —Xia, Shang and Zhou—depict not only the early creation of states but interesting views of leadership. The founders of new dynasties—Yu, Tang and King Wu—are always primarily concerned with the welfare of the people, controlled in their self-indulgences, and often favoured by heaven. When King Tang of Shang asked Yi how he could strengthen his rule, Yi replied, "Cultivate your moral character and resolve to work for the benefit of the people. Enlist in your service men of virtue and ability. Rule your domain with humanity and justice."

The stories tend to centre around three main issues: the corruption of kings, the virtue of kings and the struggle for power. Psychology and war strategies, portraits of virtuous counsellors and the dangers of beautiful concubines—all create a lively picture of those dynasties in prerecorded history.

King Yu was the founder of the Xia Dynasty after the flood. The dynasty evolves through several corrupt leaders and reaches the apex of decadence with the last ruler, King Jie. In *Biographies of Famous Women*, Liu Xiang describes Jie's wine pools and forests hung with meat, where Jie retired for months at a time, ignoring his official duties. He was said to have kept three thousand dancing girls and to have thought himself invincible as the sun.

At this time the powerful Shang State was rising, led by King Tang. King Jie was conquered and thus the Xia Dynasty fell to the Shang. However, the Shang Dynasty too evolved into decadence with its final ruler. The Shang king only wished to carouse with the famous concubine Da Ji and eventually succumbed to the invasion of King Wu, founder of the Zhou Dynasty.

The Western Zhou Dynasty, established by King Wu, too, finally evolved towards corruption, culminating in the last Western Zhou ruler, King You. Just to please his concubine, You would light his war beacon fires so often that when he was truly under attack and lit the fires, no one would come.

Our story ends here, at the end of the Western Zhou Dynasty with the beginning of written records. This chapter presents some of the most famous tales of the strength and weaknesses of kings, of their concubines and counsellors, of the rise and fall of dynasties.

The Xia Dynasty

Qi Usurps State Power

During the time of the great flood, Bo Yi was one of Yu's top officials in the arduous journey to open rivers, clear mountains and drain marshes. When the task seemed most impossible, Bo Yi was always at Yu's elbow; they laboured and struggled together, and their sweat fell as from one body and mingled with the muddy waters of the flood.

Bo Yi was a divine descendant of the swallow. Before serving Yu, he had served King Sun as minister of birds, beasts, grass and trees because he understood the language of all nature. One day, when he was digging a pit to trap wild animals, he smelled water. He dug deeper and deeper until water bubbled out of the earth, and thus he discovered the first well. He taught the people how to make wells and save the toil of carrying heavy buckets on long, springing water poles. In those days a dragon used to hide below the earth in deep underground streams, but when the people began to dig wells, the dragon escaped and was followed by all its descendants to Mount Kunlun.

As King Yu grew older, he began to plan for his successor. According to the *Book of Mountains and Seas*, Yu's son Qi was a man of unusual birth who had some divine powers. It is said that two snakes hung from his ears and he rode two dragons in three layers of clouds, wearing a spherical jade pendant on his chest. He is depicted as holding a feathered umbrella in his left hand and a jade hoop in his right. But Yu thought his son Qi to be a pleasure-seeking man and not fit to lead the people. So he named his loyal official Bo Yi as successor to the throne, and his own son Qi became only a minor palace official.

This assignment was a great humiliation to Qi. Many who love pleasure seek the power to justify their own weakness. Like Dan Zhu, the son of Yao, Qi resented his father's decision. But Qi was like unforged iron, untempered in the fire. He submitted to his father's will, biding his time until Yu would die.

When finally the old man was gone, Qi had forgotten neither his ambitions nor his humiliation. He was born from a stone with strange abilities; his great love of luxury was matched only by his great cunning and native intelligence. While the people were still mourning their king, the son began to devise a plan to usurp state power.

Qi recruited men secretly, promising vast rewards for their treachery; he bought horses and stowed provisions. In short, he built himself an army and prepared himself for war.

But Bo Yi, who now had the right to the throne, was accustomed to court intrigues. The king's death had made him wary of Qi. He knew there was a threat of conflict with Qi, a threat he had felt growing stronger as the old king grew weaker. So, in haste, Bo Yi led a group of his own men away, hoping to undermine Qi's challenge by moving the capital from Anyi to the north of Jishan Mountain.

Bo Yi's strategy was poor. The people felt deserted by their new king. And he underestimated his opponent. Alone in the old palace Qi restrained his indulgences for a time, neither drinking nor carousing during long nights. He took advantage of the resources of the old capital and made promises to the people, who through the tears of mourning saw a strange, unexpected likeness of the father in the son. They believed him, and thought to regain the benevolence of their favourite king through his blood descendant. Dukes in vassal states also praised and put their trust in him. Qi curried their shifting loyalties and made false accusations against Bo Yi. When the time was ripe, he marched with his well-fed troops to Jishan Mountain. Bo Yi had made no preparations. His men were hungry and carried few weapons; they were of the old guard who had loved the old king. But love for a dead man is nothing against the hate of the living son, and Bo Yi lost power. After a few small skirmishes his camp was broken and his men scattered. Bo Yi, ashamed of failing his dead monarch's last wish, walked into the fray and was killed.

So it was that Qi succeeded to the throne.

Now the son Qi had a wily nature, and he feared the people's memory of Bo Yi's dedication to them during the flood. To gain their confidence he established periods of sacrifice twice a year to honour Bo Yi. And so the people in double mourning were deceived.

But Qi was not long on the throne before he returned to his old ways of indulgence and pleasure-seeking. He ascended three times to the heavens as the Divine Emperor's guest, and remembering the divine music he heard there—the "Jiubian" and the "Jiuge"—he returned to earth and composed an earthly copy called the "Jiuzhao". Then at Tianmu, a mountain more than one thousand *zhang* high, he ordered his musicians to rehearse the heavenly strains. Much pleased, Qi composed lyrics and a dance and called together young girls to perform and boys to wave ox tails. In a pleasure palace called Dalezhiye to the north of Dayun Mountain Qi lounged on his dragons, floated on the clouds and watched his spectacle through the shifting mists and green trees of the peaks. It is said that he even took his father Yu's nine famous vessels from in front of the palace where they were displayed to teach the people. They had divine powers and needed no fire for cooking; Qi used them as common cauldrons in which to prepare his delicacies and heat his wine.

As his father Yu had suspected, Qi was a worthless king who cared little for his people and defied their will. Blindly they had turned their faces to young Qi's deception, and now they suffered under him. But sometimes heaven makes unexpected retributions.

Qi fathered five sons who grew up much influenced by his example. They were unruly and lazy; they fought frequently with each other and learned nothing of state affairs. Qi despaired of controlling them and instead sought refuge in his clouds. When he died, the five boys, who knew loyalty to neither brother nor father, neither king nor state, divided up their grandfather Yu's great kingdom into five small portions. Each brother inherited his own small territory, dividing not only the land but the people, and frequently disputing with neighbouring brothers.

At this time there was only one official to whom people could turn for justice. His name was Meng Tu, a strange half-man, half-god with magic powers. To judge a dispute he would open his eyes very wide and stare at the plaintiff and the accused. Then a blood stain would mysteriously appear on the clothes of one of the two in dispute and Meng Tu would pronounce the one with the blood stain guilty. The people respected the official, but he could do little in a country divided into five parts with five unruly leaders.

Even iron is weak if shredded too fine, and watching the turmoil from a nearby state, King Hou Yi seized his chance. When the brothers had divided the land, he led his troops into one territory after another, and easily he conquered these tiny divided lands, and easily he seized power.

Hou Yi of Youqiong State

Hou Yi was the son of a simple peasant. He was still a baby swinging in his cradle when he asked for his first bow. He had been sleeping in the sun, and flies were buzzing around his face. His father gave him a tiny bow and tiny arrows, and the child picked them up and immediately shot ten flies dead.

As a child his favourite hero was the divine archer Yi. The boy practised with his tiny bow and arrow, and began to call himself Yi. So the people too began to call him Hou Yi (Later Yi), or King Yi, and that was his name.

One day when the boy was five years old, his parents took him with them to pick healing herbs on a nearby mountain. Cicadas buzzed in the trees; the day was hot and dusty. After the long trek into the forest the child was too tired to move. He grew heavy in his parents' arms, and so they decided to leave him to sleep until they were finished picking the herbs. They found a tree in which only a single cicada sang. Here they thought to find their son again among all the trees of the dense mountain forest.

By twilight they had finished their digging and gathering. As they hurried back into the darkening forest, they were horrified to see that swarms of cicadas buzzed loudly from every tree and their child was not to be found. Deep mountain darkness fell over the place, and Hou Yi's parents grew frantic. They searched everywhere, tracing countless paths through the pine needles. Finally when it was too dark to see anything they returned home, only to rise again next day with the sun and return to search on the mountain. For days they grieved and searched, but all to no avail. The child Yi was nowhere to be found.

On that afternoon, Hou Yi had awoken to the buzz of the cicadas. The mountain seemed a wonderful place to him, and he chased butterflies and played in the streams and collected coloured pebbles until dark. But when the long shadows gathered, so did his doubts, and he went to the side of a path and sat on a big boulder, crying silently, waiting for his parents.

After a while he heard heavy footsteps. Those feet belonged to the hunter Chu Hufu, who lived alone in the mountains. He saw the boy sitting all alone and asked the child where he lived. But little Hou Yi was so overwhelmed with fear that he could only mutely shake his head, tears rolling down his face and dropping from his chin. So the hunter took him along and adopted him as his son.

Chu Hufu was an excellent archer, and as the child grew he learned the skills of archery from his adoptive father. The man noticed that the lad's left arm was longer than his right, something which allowed him to pull his bow even more curved and strong.

When Hou Yi was twenty, the hunter suddenly died and the boy was once more left alone. He stood on a cliff and pulling his bowstring back, he lifted his arrow to the sky and cried out, "Let me begin to take a path of power in the world; let this arrow lead me back to my old home."

With that he let fly the arrow.

It traced a great arc into the sky, and as Yi watched it fell to the ground. He was amazed! It did not pierce the earth but slid through the grasses like a snake. The arrow traced a path through the forest, curving round the mountainside and finally heading out into a clearing. Hou Yi ran behind, on and on over a great distance to a side of the mountain he thought never to have seen before. For a moment he lost track of the trail, and then suddenly he saw the arrow lodged in the threshold of an old, ramshackle hut overgrown with vines. Pushing open the broken door, he found a few shards of pottery and cobwebs. He came back outside, blinking into the bright sunlight, and walked until he found a neighbouring hut. To those people he asked the question he feared to ask: "Friends, who lived in that hut in the clearing there beyond the copse?"

"Why stranger," replied the old man, "a poor old man and his wife who long ago lost their only son in the mountains. They lived there until they died a year ago. . ." The peasant scrutinized the young man standing before him. "One might think by the line of your jaw that you were the old man himself, so great is your resemblance."

And so Hou Yi knew that his arrow had led him home.

It is said that he tried to live there, but he knew neither how to weave cloth nor how to cultivate the land. So Hou Yi picked up his bow and his quiver of arrows and set out to roam the earth.

During his wandering he met an archery master by the name of Wu He. Seeing the lad's natural skill, the man took him as his student and began to teach him. They wandered, shooting together, Wu He encouraging his apprentice. One day they saw a small bird in the sky and Wu He said, "Shoot it through the left eye."

Hou Yi raised his bow, aimed and let fly the arrow. The bird stopped in mid-flight and fell heavily to the ground. Together the master and the student walked over to their prey. The arrow had pierced the bird's eye, but it was the right one. And the teacher said: "Not bad."

But Hou Yi blushed in shame. He practised harder and harder until his arrows flew like lightning, deadly accurate as the swift flight of an eagle.

He roamed about ridding the people of dangerous beasts and scourges, and the people loved him and honoured him. His reputation preceded him everywhere he wandered, and one day as he was walking in the State of Youqiong, the people knew he was coming and they went out to greet him. They asked him to be their king.

Hou Yi had not long been king when he heard of the internal strife between the five brothers of the neighbouring state. Their continual battling was creating misery among the people in the State of Xia. And so Hou Yi gathered his troops, marched in and took over that land. His fame had already reached the ears of the Xia people, and they rallied to him to rid themselves of the tyrannical pleasure-seekers who had set themselves up as kings. Thus Hou Yi became chief over princes and ruler of the powerful expanded State of Youqiong on the central plain.

Now such was the presence and fame of Hou Yi that all the princes and dukes of the minor states obeyed his orders with the exception of one hot-tempered man named Bo Feng. Bo Feng was the son of Kui, an official of music in Yao's kingdom. He had a black, fleshy piglike face and was so greedy and stubborn that people called him Big Boar. His mother, Xuan Qi, was a great beauty, the daughter of You Rengshi, and although she was no longer young, she wore long thick tresses down her back so that the people called her Black Fox.

Hou Yi would not tolerate any disobedience, and he took his troops to fight the upstart Bo Feng. With some regret he watched Big Boar on the battlefield. The man was a skilful fighter, but knowing he could never win the loyalty of one so stubborn, Hou Yi raised his bow and shot Big Boar through the head.

Hou Yi and his men marched back in glory to Big Boar's kingdom. Inside the city, Hou Yi saw Big Boar's frightened mother and fell deeply in love. The woman looked in horror upon this man who had murdered her son. She alone mourned and wept for him. Her state was broken. Her son was dead. She tried to retire out of sight, but Hou Yi would have nothing but the mother's hand in marriage. How he longed for that beautiful woman, the Black Fox. And so, ignoring the derision of the people and of his men, Hou Yi pursued her. The woman, Xuan Qi, had no one left in the world, and she dared not object to the new king. Swallowing her silent tears of mourning, she succumbed to him and pretended to obey her new lord Hou Yi, but all the while she furtively watched for her chance to avenge her son.

On the way back home Hou Yi was approached by a young man, a son of a feudal prince called Han Zhuo, who had come from the distant State of Hai to seek refuge with the famous archer. He was a cunning and wicked man whose fair-minded father had ignored him. But he sought power and would not accept this rejection. He too had heard of King Yi and met him just returning from the State of Xia, drunk with victory, a beautiful new wife in his entourage. Proud Yi was easily pleased by the flattery of the smooth-tongued Han Zhuo and took him in as a trusted follower.

By the time they reached the palace, Hou Yi, full of his own power, had appointed Han Zhuo his prime minister and banished for ever his wise and faithful officials Wu Luo, Bo Ying, Xiong Kun and Pang Yu. After the defeat of Big Boar, he considered his authority inviolable, his own judgement indisputable. He, after all, ruled the world. And he began to abandon state affairs, taking his guards out into the fields to hunt. The tedious state business he left with the honey-tongued official Han Zhuo.

When ambition and deception meet, they find in each other good bedfellows. Han Zhuo craftily took more and more power; Hou Yi's wife meanwhile was looking for a chance of revenge. During the king's absences on those long afternoons of hunting, the king's wife and the king's prime minister dallied together and soon they began to plot against him.

On the day they first whispered to each other that they wanted to murder the king, Xuan Qi drew Han Zhuo close to her and whispered in his ear, "A bird must strengthen his wings to soar in the sky, when you are ready I will be your gust of wind."

Han Zhuo listened and heeded her advice. He began to cultivate powerful henchmen and sought new support from the people. Wearing the mask of an honest man, all of his own official mistakes he attributed to the absent Hou Yi.

Han Zhuo urged his king to hunt and secretly instructed the beautiful queen to be capricious and demanding. Nothing Hou Yi could do would please the woman he loved and he grew moody, flying into rages with the maidservants, beating his imperial bodyguards. Those who were mistreated began to hate their king, and Han Zhuo seized the moment of their wavering affections to draw them to his side with soft words and promises.

And so was Hou Yi deceived in an intrigue against him plotted by his prime minister and his wife.

One night returning from the hunt with his bodyguards, Hou Yi suddenly heard the whizz of an arrow and felt fire in his shoulder. He turned his head sharply; three, four, five more arrows from behind and in front knocked him off his horse. He was mortally wounded and could not raise himself up. Out of the woods dashed Han Zhuo and his followers. Those few fighting bodyguards who had not been informed of the plot and tried to fight for their king were quickly cut to the ground.

There is no violence like that unleashed with the usurpation of power. The guards hoisted the dripping corpse above their heads and made a wild torchlit procession back to the castle. Throwing the body down at the feet of the queen, they roared and drank and named Han Zhuo their king and Xuan Qi his queen. Then they lit a huge fire and dumped the body of Hou Yi into a cauldron of boiling water. They brought the young son of Hou Yi's first wife into the feasting room and tried to make him drink the broth of his father. And when the boy refused, they bound him and dragged him to the gate of the capital and murdered him there in the street for all to see.

So it was that Han Zhuo succeeded Hou Yi as king of the State of Youqiong. His new wife Xuan Qi bore him two sons called Jiao and Yi, who grew up strong and powerful. With their father they soon entered into a complicit tyranny of all who opposed them.

The people mourned the late king Hou Yi. They hated the violent, greedy gang and waited only for a chance to rise up against them. And of course, Shao Kang, the grandson of Qi, was watching these events with great interest. His father and four uncles had been driven from the state, and Shao Kang deprived of his land. He decided that now the empire was once again vulnerable enough to be overthrown.

When Shao Kang set out for the capital he had only five hundred soldiers and horses, while the tyrannical Han Zhuo and his two sons guarded strategic positions with massive troops. However, it was not long before the brave Shao Kang defeated Han Zhuo's army.

Thus it was that with the eclipse of the State of Youqiong, the Xia Dynasty could rise again.

Kong Jia, Lover of Dragons

After Shao Kang took over, the Xia Dynasty passed through a dozen generations until the reign of King Kong Jia. Once again the central authority had achieved sufficient strength to allow a king to neglect his official duties. King Kong Jia believed in fairies and ghosts. He loved to hunt and to dally with women, to wrap himself in silk and to eat exotic delicacies. With each indulgence the prestige and virtue of the Xia Dynasty fell. The emperor no longer inspired the people. Princes fell away, disobedient, despising their indulgent and weak ruler.

Kong Jia loved best of all to hunt. One day he called together his bodyguards, his hunting dogs and falcons, and set out for the mountain inhabited by the god of luck, Tai Feng. The god of luck had long been displeased by Kong Jia, so he called for winds to blow the imperial hunters away. Suddenly the men were beset by a wild storm, and stones and sand whirled through the air. The hunting group scattered, and the king and a few men who stayed near him lost their way.

Kong Jia and his bodyguards wandered over the mountain until they found a small peasant's hut in a sheltered part of the valley. It so happened that a new child had been born to the household that night. The king was invited to sit along one wall, drinking a warm wine grog, the best the house could offer. He acknowledged the respectful greetings paid to him and listened to the friends and relatives congratulating the new parents.

Some said, "What a lucky day for the child's birth! Meeting the king after only a few hours on earth marks a fortunate future."

But others disagreed, shaking their heads and talking among themselves: "It may be a lucky day, but it will not establish his future. We must look out for him and take precautions against his suffering in times to come."

At these words the king rose up in fury. "Nonsense!" he shouted. "I will take this baby and raise him as my son. We will see who dares to bring suffering to a prince."

So the winds calmed and Kong Jia strode out of the house and back to his palace. In due time when the child was old enough, two men returned to the peasant's house to fetch the boy back. And a plan formed in the king's mind. To prove his power to shape the joy and suffering of anyone he pleased, he decided to make the boy a fine official. With a show of finery and a fierce presence he thought anyone could be an official. So he gave the child neither special knowledge nor skills, but simply waited until he was tall enough to fit the official robes.

But even a king cannot control fate, and it was fate that thwarted his desires.

One day the boy was playing in the arms practice hall of the palace when suddenly a strong gust of wind swept a heavy curtain down from the inside eaves. With a crash the fold of cloth hit a rack of weapons, sending it flying through the air. The boy jumped and dodged away from the falling weapons. But a flying axe fell squarely down and chopped off one of his feet. The boy in whom the king had placed all his hopes was suddenly maimed.

Now, this boy had been taught nothing and prepared for nothing in life. The king decided a maimed official could never command respect, and so he made the lad an ordinary doorkeeper. He sighed to himself over fate and composed a song entitled "Song of the Chopping Axe", which is said to be the earliest song of the eastern realms.

One of Kong Jia's great loves was raising dragons. Now in China the dragon has a divine nature, and it is said that Yu, first monarch of the Xia Dynasty, was himself a dragon. Thanks to the dragon Ying Long, Yu was able to regulate the waters. Other dragons later appeared to congratulate Yu. Once King Shun dug out hairy dragons from a vein in the earth in the State of Nanxun, and these he kept in a special place, the "dragon-feeding palace" Such anecdotes suggest to us the close relationship between leaders of the Xia Dynasty and dragons.

Kong Jia was fond of dragons and kept two, a female and a male. Lacking knowledge on the needs and desires of dragons, he sought out someone particularly skilled in their care. And finally one day a man called Liu Lei presented himself as a dragon keeper at the court.

Liu Lei was a descendant of King Yao. But his family had fallen and he had no permanent work or position in the state. When he heard of the king's need, he went to an old dragon tamer, an exemplary man called Huan Long who was a descendant of the dragon-feeding official of King Shun's time. Liu Lei stayed with Huan Long a few days, learning only the most rudimentary knowledge. Then he hurried to the king, who believed his foolish flattery and self-promotion. Kong Jia gave him the title "imperial dragon tender", and Liu Lei, the son of a fallen aristocrat, was very pleased to be back at court again.

Liu Lei's ignorance of his professed skill, however, was quickly apparent when the female dragon died. He should have quaked at his mistake, but arrogantly he ordered his men to drag the dead dragon out of the pool, to take away her scales and guts, then to

chop up the meat and cook it. This meat he offered to the king as wild venison from his own hunting.

The foolish king ate the meat for several days, thinking it very delicious. Soon he called for his official to arrange a dragon spectacle for him. Of course Liu Lei could do nothing but have the lackadaisical male dragon perform all alone. He made excuses for the female, but the king became suspicious. Several times he asked to see the female dragon, and each time he met with an excuse. Finally one evening in a rage the king demanded to see the dragon. Liu Lei knew there could be no more stalling, so he gathered together a bundle of his things. That night, he stealthily crept out of the palace and ran away to Luxian County, never to be seen again.

Now the king found himself again in his old dilemma: he needed a dragon keeper. At last an old master of the skill, Shi Men, presented himself. Shi Men had fairy powers; he ate plum and peach flowers, and like Chi Songzi and Ning Fengzhi of ancient times, he could temper himself to grow light in a fire and ascend to the heavens.

One thing Shi Men knew was dragons. He could make Kong Jia's dance joyfully into the air, leaping and curling through the sky. The king was pleased and began to show more and more interest in his pet. He loitered at the dragon feeding palace and began to suggest new methods of feeding and training. But sometimes arrogance accompanies knowledge. Shi Men was a dragon expert and he ridiculed the king. Unlike his flattering predecessor he mocked the king's ideas. And one day he went too far.

Kong Jia came to the skilled trainer one day and said: "Let us tie long golden streamers to the dragon's tail."

But Shi Men sniffed indignantly and refused. Kong Jia was suddenly enraged and ordered his head cut off at the palace gates.

But Shi Men only laughed heartily and said: "There's no use in cutting off my head—you will still be defeated."

Then he was dragged out between two guards.

Not long after, his bloody head was brought back for the king's inspection. The king feared that Shi Men's spirit would haunt the place, and so he commanded his men to carry the corpse and the head away and bury them deep in the wilderness.

Hardly was the last shovel of dirt thrown over the body in the shallow grave when a great storm blew up. A fire roared through the forest and flames swept across the sky.

Watching from a palace tower, Kong Jia shuddered to see fire burst out in the very direction he had buried the dead dragon keeper. Who knows what power this spirit had! Perhaps those flames would leap back and envelop the palace too. He called for his cart to carry him to the man's grave, and there he prayed.

Gradually the flames subsided. But only when the fire was cold ash did Kong Jia relax and climb back up into his cart. He motioned the driver to take him home.

No one knows what happened between that shallow grave and the palace. The men who accompanied the cart all claim that nothing at all unusual took place on the path home. All we know is that something happened. When the imperial guard stepped forward to open the door of the cart, he saw the king sitting motionless. Gently he reached in to awaken his monarch and was horrified to feel the body cold and already stiff. No one knows exactly what happened after the strange fire and the prayer at the dragon keeper's grave. The truth is that the king was dead.

Jie, Last King of the Xia Dynasty

With the passing of Kong Jia, his great-grandson Lu Gui succeeded him. His new name and title were King Jie of Xia, and he of all kings is notorious in Chinese folklore for his debauches and tyranny.

King Jie of Xia was a broadly-built man, handsome and powerful. He could snap the antler of a deer with one twist of his hand and could straighten iron hooks between his fingers. He plunged into waters to fight fearsome dragons with his bare hands; he battled jackals, wolves, tigers and leopards. From all outward appearances he seemed a man of exceptional ability, a man with the qualities of a hero. But at the core of his being lay a false and corrupt heart.

He had a magnificent palace built for himself by the tears and sweat of his people; he called it Yaotai. There he hoarded treasures and beautiful maidens from throughout the country. There he kept his idle flatterers as servants and a troupe of dancers and dwarfs to amuse him. Some say there were three thousand dancing girls alone.

Not far from one of the palace buildings he had his men dig an enormous pond where a half dozen boats could float, and he filled it with wine. They say that to the frenzied beating of drums Jie would have three thousand people lie flat by the pool and drink together. Some fell drunk and drowned in the sweet liquid, and the king and his favourite queen, Mei Xi, would laugh together.

The most infamous palace built by King Jie was located in a secret valley and called the Eternal Night Palace. Through the gates of that palace favoured aristocrats passed and disappeared for weeks on end. While King Jie was in the Eternal Night Palace, he would neglect state affairs.

One night a terrible windstorm arose, tossing stones and sand in the air and burying the palace of pleasure. It happened that the king was not staying there that night, but some people interpreted this storm as a sign from heaven. When they expressed their fears to him, he scoffed and said he had no time for the whining of fools.

The queen Mei Xi had a peculiar fetish of her own: she loved the sound of silk tearing. King Jie of Xia would order his attendants to bring out shimmering bolts of the finest silks to tear before the queen and amuse her.

One time, a young imperial maid suddenly turned into a fierce dragon. Her head began to stretch, and fangs sprang out of her mouth. Long claws erupted from her fingernails, which she brandished through the air. Everyone in the court was terrified, and no one dared approach her. But then, just as suddenly, she took the shape of a beautiful, unassuming woman. Only King Jie was not afraid of this creature. He made a pet of her and loved her. When she began to crave men to eat, he ordered human flesh served to her. He called her Jiao Qie, which means "dragon concubine", and she was thought to be able to see into the future.

In those days, officials who tried to fulfil their true function and advise the king lived in constant danger of their lives. One wise man, Guan Longfeng, could not bear to see the king's licentious debauchery and criticized him quite frankly.

But the king was enraged and had the man jailed and executed.

King Jie had another official called Yi Yin who had once served King Tang of the Yin (another name for Shang) Dynasty. Yi Yin felt that King Tang had never fully recognized his abilities, nor offered him high enough positions, so he came to King Jie and served as an imperial official in the kitchen. This is his story:

In the east there was once a state called Youshen. One day, in that place, a young girl took a basket to the woods to gather mulberry leaves. As she wandered peacefully along, she heard a baby's cry. She followed the sound to an old hollow mulberry tree, where she found a chubby, red-faced baby. It was a curious thing indeed, but the girl gently lifted the child into her basket and took him to her prince. He asked his cooks to raise him and sent some men out to make inquiries about the abandoned child. Not long after, they returned with this account. The boy's mother lived on the banks of the Yishui River, and one night when she was pregnant, a god had appeared to her in a dream, saying, "If the rice-husking mortar swells with water, then turn eastward and never look back."

The very next day that god's words came true. She saw water oozing from her stone mortar. At once she consulted with her neighbours and asked them to go east with her. Some people believed the woman and followed; but others, doubting, stayed in their homes.

They had travelled only ten *li* eastward when the woman, worried about her friends left behind, turned round to look once again at her old hometown. She was horrified to see the place submerged in flood waters, and no sooner had she looked than did great waves rush towards the little band of people trying to escape. The woman held out her frail hand as if to push back the torrents, but paralysed she could neither move nor cry out. Suddenly she changed into an old hollow mulberry tree that stolidly resisted the flood.

And after some time those treacherous waters fell back.

So it happened that the child was discovered in that same tree. The king's officials told all this to the king, and the boy was brought up in the kitchens of the State of Yi and called Yi Yin, which means "Yi official". He was clever and became a master cook and was made an imperial teacher for the daughter of the King of Youshen.

Now some time later when King Tang was travelling eastward through that state, he heard of the beautiful and virtuous daughter of the King of Youshen and he asked to marry her. Knowing the fine reputation of King Tang, the King of Youshen agreed and the marriage took place. According to the custom of that time, the new wife followed her husband back to his own State of Yin.

The boy Yi Yin wanted also to go and serve King Tang. He felt that his abilities were wasted in the king's kitchens. He sought an audience with the King of Youshen and asked to be allowed to accompany the young bride as her dowry official. The king did not think much of the young dark-skinned man brought to him from a hollow mulberry tree, and he let him go.

So Yi Yin followed along with the bride and King Tang. He carried a special cauldron and a chopping board, and King Tang soon learned of his talent as a cook. He was given a chance to prepare a meal, and the young man produced such exquisite delicacies that the king agreed to grant an audience to Yi Yin.

The people helped prepare him for his audience with the highest official of the land. They feared that beneath his courtly appearance lay certain evils left from his mysterious and lowly background, so they bathed him and smoked him with burning sweetgrass. According to the ancient Chinese notion that evil can drive away evil, he was painted with the blood of oxen and pigs. They thus made him ready to see the king.

Yi Yin thought his chance had finally arrived. He went to the palace and spoke eloquently of everything from unusual cuisine to affairs of state administration. King Tang heard him out. He thought him capable and ambitious, indeed different from other cooks, but he somehow did not promote him.

The young man was disappointed. And so, as was the custom in those days when a man sought advancement, he left King Tang and went to King Jie to seek a better position. With King Jie he became official of the imperial kitchen and hoped for quick advancement.

Now Yi Yin was an intelligent man and truly sought the welfare of the people. One night he was with the king and his

sycophants at Yaotai, and he saw the king amusing himself with his lewd company. That night Yi Yin decided it was time to speak up, and he proposed a toast: "If Your Excellency does not listen to me, the state will soon be ruined."

The king slammed the table with his fist. But something rang true in Yi Yin's words and so, half-drunk, the king defended himself: "You spread lies to deceive the people. I rule the world as the sun shines over it. Whoever questions the sun? When the sun forgets to rise, then will my state be ruined. So you see . . . fool . . . stop your foolish talk!"

Jie was a proud man and often referred to himself as "father of heaven". He loved to compare his state to the sun, and indeed he moved around, comparing himself to the sun. But in his corruption he had neglected his people and he had no knowledge of what they said. Cursing him, they cried out, "Detested sun! Die, die light! I would rather die with you."

So Yi Yin watched the king obstinately cling to his carousing and waste, and he left grimly to return home. On the street, he saw a group of people half-drunk, stumbling and holding each other up. They were singing a strange song:

Why not go to Bo?
Why not go to Bo?
Bo is strong enough.

The song seemed to echo from the eaves of the houses. It was repeated over and over as if all the streets and lanes were singing.

Yi Yin was surprised because Bo had been his own old capital, the home of King Tang whom he had left. Could it be true that his former king was really worthy and wise?

Turning into his doorway he climbed up the steps, and yet another song drifted through the window from a distant alley:

Awake, awake,
Decided is my fate.
Away from darkness
to the light.
Awake, awake!

Yi Yin's troubled brow suddenly cleared. The song, of course, was intended for him. It had been a mistake to leave the kitchen of a good king to be an official for a wicked one. And with that he gathered his belongings, ordered up a mule cart, and left the capital of Jie of Xia to return to Bo, the capital of his former king, Tang.

One of King Jie's trusted followers was a man called Fei Chang. One day as he was strolling on the bank of the Yellow River, he noticed two suns in the sky, one rising brilliantly in the east amid coloured clouds, the other setting into a grey mist in the west. Terrible thunder echoed from the heavens, and Fei Chang was deeply troubled by the strange power of these signs.

He thought to himself, "There cannot be two suns in the sky; the people cannot be governed by two monarchs."

He turned towards the water and asked He Bo, god of the rivers, "Which of the suns is the State of Xia, and which is the State of Yin?"

And the god answered, "The sun in the west is Xia; the sun in the east is Yin."

The sign was bad indeed: Xia State would not last much longer. So, like Yi Yin, the official Fei Chang also took his family and went to serve King Tang because it is true that one mouth cannot tell two stories at the same time. So it was that such loyal followers as Fei Chang were forced to leave the Xia kingdom sinking in the west and turn their faces to the rising State of Yin in the east.

The Shang Dynasty

The Yin Nation: Herders and Princes

Di Ku, the god of the east, had two wives who lived in a tower. The one called Jian Di swallowed a bird's egg and gave birth to Qi, father of the Yin nation. Qi had helped Yu control the flood and was later an official of education for King Shun at Shang. In time King Tang moved his capital to Bo, and a dozen generations later King Pan Geng settled his capital at Yin. So Yin became another name for the Shang Dynasty.

Several generations before King Tang, the Yin were a nomadic nation living in the eastern grasslands led by Prince Hai. Prince Hai was skilled at animal husbandry; his cows were strong and fat, his herds of sheep covered the lower fields. The people learned his methods, and soon their sleek herds increased and covered the wilderness. Enjoying this abundance, the prince devised a plan to make his people even richer and discussed it with his younger brother Wang Heng. He knew of a nation on the other side of the Yellow River called Youyi. These people were prosperous farmers who had great stores of wheat and made fine silks. Why not make an exchange with the foreigners—cows and sheep for wheat and cloth? In that way all the people would benefit.

The plan was a good one, and with the consent of the people, the two brothers gathered together some of their best herds and selected sturdy young men to help them make the journey. The colourful group set out with high expectations, and when they reached the water, the river god He Bo, who was a friend to the states on both his sides, guided them safely across the treacherous river.

The prince of Youyi State, Mian Chen, soon heard that guests from the east were approaching his home. He went personally to welcome them, offering a lavish banquet such as the grassland nomads had never seen. How they enjoyed the wine and music and dancing! When one follows the flocks, there is little time to develop such arts.

So the herdsmen remained there enjoying a life of ease in the State of Youyi, growing round and fat, the hard muscles of their loins growing soft.

The elder brother was distinguished as much by his taciturnity as by his great appetite. One record describes him hoisting with both hands the head of an enormous wild bird into his mouth and chomping energetically. He had great bushy eyebrows over brooding eyes and would sit planted like an old stump at banquets eating and drinking as if he were all alone. The rest of the day he tended the herds and picked wild plants, as restless and vigorous as the grassland winds themselves.

The younger brother, Wang Heng, had a good appetite too. But his eyes hungered after beautiful women. Entranced by the women in this place, he found that the most exquisite person in

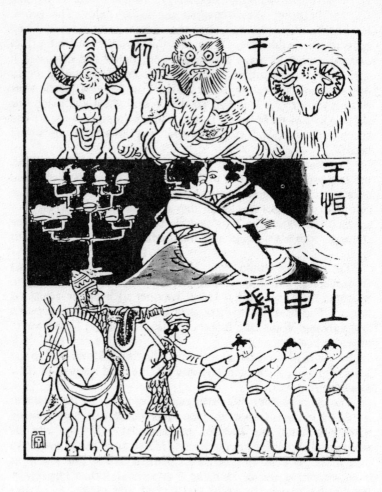

the whole country was none other than the wife of King Mian
Chen. Young Prince Wang Heng had had many love affairs, and
now he tried his amorous arts before the queen. The frivolous
woman was bored by her ageing husband, and secretly they began
to meet. But it takes more subtlety than that of a rough herdsman
to keep the attentions of a queen. She soon tired of Wang Heng;
many bees like him had offered her nectar from the flowers. Her
restless eyes began wandering again and were caught by the quiet
mystery of his elder brother, Prince Hai. The art of the queen's
love was practised and ingenious; it was not long before the
inexperienced Prince Hai was captive to her delights. The cool
nature of the young man was quickly aroused by her fire, and
soon all the court knew of their passion except the old husband
Mian Chen.

The first to learn of the affair was the younger brother. He
had never expected his own flesh to steal his new prize. When
naïve Prince Hai confessed to his younger brother that he had
tasted a great love, he never suspected that his brother knew of
her pleasures too. And for his part the young Wang Heng thought
court rumours would have whispered of his own affair. But
neither brother understood. The knife of jealousy wielded by the
hand of fraternal rage is dangerous indeed. Behind the younger
brother's smiling congratulations his jaw was tight.

And all the while yet another man was watching. The imperial
bodyguard of Prince Mian Chen had also dallied with the king's
wife before the arrival of the two foreign princes. But her door
had been shut to him of late, and the young warrior was deeply
shamed. He sought an opportunity for revenge and soon found it
in the younger brother Wang Heng.

The two began to discuss a scheme to deal with their common
rival. Wang Heng simply wanted to murder his elder brother with
a borrowed knife. But the bodyguard wanted to protect the
honour of his small nation from the taint of this dusty prince.
Together they plotted, united not by friendship but by the bond
of hatred.

Wang Heng could easily spy on his brother; the strong bodyguard would wield the murder weapon.

One moonlit night the elder brother Prince Hai stumbled back
drunk from a hunting expedition and entered the back door of

the palace. Wang Heng was watching and hurried to inform the bodyguard. The young man nodded silently, hid a sharp hand axe in his coat, and walked stealthily through the familiar back halls of the palace. Stealing into the drawing room of the queen, he looked through a window at the fat man snoring on the queen's bed. Infuriated, he rushed through the unlocked door and brought his axe down on the sleeping man's neck. Blood spurted out like a fountain, and with another slash the head rolled away loose. But in the murderer's eyes the foreign prince's body still glistened; his very blood seemed to hold the beauty of the twilight sun and coloured clouds; he seemed to smell of the sweet grasslands and a vision of gently grazing sheep. The murderer was maddened with the sight. He slashed again and again, opening the head into two pieces down the centre of the face, dividing eye from eye and ear from ear. He hacked off the prince's arms and legs, and his fury was not abated until seven parts of the body lay scattered round the bloody room.

When he looked at the scene of devastation he suddenly remembered again who he was. He wiped off the axe and sought his escape—but too late, too late! Some imperial maids awakened by his fury had witnessed the scene and now began to scream, "Murder! Murder!"

Armed guards rushed from the courtyard and caught the young man. They dragged him to the panic-stricken old king. The king sat up in bed beside his queen, who only moments before had slipped from the bed where Prince Hai lay slaughtered.

The inquiry began, but the truth was only partly disclosed. Enraged at the foreign philanderer, King Mian Chen ordered Hai's herds and herdsmen seized. He expelled the brother Wang Heng and pardoned the bodyguard. Only the queen's position remained to be determined. She pleaded and wept, blaming the seductions of her lover. Finally the king softened and placed all the blame on the murdered prince. So the herdsmen's dreams of wealth and pleasure melted away like ice.

But now Prince Wang Heng was in a difficult position. He had to return to his state alone, without brother, herds, or foreign goods. After the long journey he strode into his home court and told of his brother's love affair, embellishing it with details for eager ears, and the people felt they had much to be indignant

about. They had lost their property and what's more, their prince.
Immediately they named Wang Heng their prince and chose
generals to lead their armies to seek revenge.

Although Prince Wang Heng had deliberately inflamed the
people to seize power, he feared to war with the northern state
lest his own part in the murder conspiracy be exposed. It was best
not to take up arms too quickly. He proposed to go north in the
spirit of negotiation. If the flocks were returned, then the herds-
people would consider all equal; if not, they would fight. Only
reluctantly did those people agree out of respect for their new
leader.

So for the second time Prince Wang Heng led a small entourage across the river to the State of Youyi. And King Mian Chen
dared not offend the well-prepared mission from the State of Yin.
They talked, and he agreed to return the herds and flocks. With
this success, Wang Heng suddenly grew proud. Yes, the flocks
should be returned, and he, such a powerful prince, should
remain here for a while to enjoy good wine, lithe dancing, and
perhaps his former lover. What need had he to return and be a
poor nomadic prince of the grasslands?

This idea in mind, Wang Heng remained at his host's table.
And according to etiquette the King of Youyi could say nothing,
but only offer his guest a second helping . . . and a third. So Prince
Wang Heng stayed until several years had passed.

Meanwhile the people of Yin were waiting. After some time
they thought that another incident must have occurred. To avoid
any further turmoil in the state, they appointed Shang Jiawei, the
son of Wang Heng, as prince. Thinking that the unknown barbar-
ians of Youyi had murdered not only his uncle but also his father,
the young prince determined to lead his troops northward.

As the mighty army approached the Yellow River, they called
out to He Bo for his help, but the river god hesitated. The nations
on both his shores were his friends, so how could he allow one of
their armies to cross and attack the other? But they cried out their
accusations, the humiliations they had suffered, the loss of two
princes and the best of their herds. What could he do? He helped
the boy lead his troops safely across the river.

When scouts reported to the King of Youyi that Shang Jiawei's troops were approaching, the old man panicked. He knew

that it must be because of Wang Heng's long stay. So he sent a diplomatic envoy to tell the true story. Shang Jiawei only half believed the story. He had travelled long; his troops were like an arrow released from the bow that can neither slow down nor return. He killed the diplomat and ordered his army forward.

The poor, aged, cuckolded king was not prepared for war. He gathered a few straggling foot soldiers together who were no match at all for the proud riders of the grasslands. The nation of Youyi was soon conquered, the capital taken and littered with dead. The old king lay silent on the ground outside the city gates.

The victorious army then poured into the capital, young Shang Jiawei wild with his first victory. He sent men to look for his father, whom he believed to have been detained all these years. But Wang Heng had disappeared, probably murdered in the skirmishes by angry Youyi people. Shang Jiawei would not be sated—he ordered a massacre and soon the state was a silent heap of bodies. The hoarse, hungry cries of the birds looking down over the orgy of death were the only sound of mourning. And the young prince led his triumphant army home.

When they reached the river, even He Bo himself dared not offend his old friends. But after they had passed with their bloody weapons and spoils, He Bo visited the fallen capital.

The once cultivated fields lay full of weeds; the looms sat stiff from want of use. Only a few old men and women had survived, hiding under dead bodies or deep in the countryside. But He Bo took mercy on this haunted remnant and gathered them into another nation and moved them to a new land. This new nation he called Yinmin (also Yaomin), and the people there were said to have a pair of long birdlike legs. These people of the Yinmin nation were considered to be the original ancestors of the people of the Qin State.

After this victory, the Yin people became very prosperous. Six or seven generations after King Shang Jiawei, King Tang set up a new capital in Bo. They did not forget their former princes. In one of their greatest sacrifices they offered a hundred cows to Wang Heng and their great-grandfather Shang Jiawei. And neither did they forget the help of the river god He Bo.

So it was that at that time the people of the grasslands came to be the most powerful nation in the east.

King Tang Defeats Jie of Xia

The son of Zhu Gui was prince Cheng Tang, a tall man with a pale face, thick hair and a handsome beard. His fine appearance was matched by his kind heart, and this is the well-known story of how he saved the birds.

Once Cheng Tang was hunting beyond the forest when he saw a man spreading out a four-sided bird net and chanting:

All the birds I call,
From the sky you fall.
No matter at all,
Every bird must fall.

But Tang objected. If he continues, all the birds will be captured! Only such a cruel man as Jie would come up with an idea like that! So Prince Tang told the man to fasten only one side of his net and he taught him a new song:

Spiders spin webs,
People set nets,
Birds soar in the sky
Up and down.
Only those fated
In my trap must die.

When the small states to the south of the Hanshui River heard of Prince Tang's compassion, they admired him and sought to follow him. Soon his kingdom included forty small states.

His neighbour King Jie of Xia was so preoccupied with his debauches that he was completely unaware of the growing force just beyond his borders. King Jie's current sport was to release wild tigers into the crowded market-place and watch the people's panic and the beasts' destruction. This grieved Prince Tang and he sent officials to offer his condolences to the bereaved families of the market-place victims. Jie of Xia was enraged at Tang's interference and saw his compassion only as an attempt to buy popular support. Then one of his slandering officials, Zhao Liang, gave him an idea. Why not issue a beautifully worded imperial edict inviting Prince Tang to the capital? And so it was done, and when the prince arrived, expecting the traditional hospitality of his host, he was roughly dragged out and clapped into Zhongquan jail. The poor prince, accustomed to court life, could hardly bear the tortures of the prison, and it was only after the people from his state bribed officials and Jie himself with treasures and precious jewels that he was finally released.

Jie now thought the time was ripe to assert his power, and he ordered his commander Bian to lead the army into the small state of Minshang in the southwest. The weakly defended territory toppled. The people were obliged to pay tribute to King Jie in the form of two beautiful women called Wan and Yan. At first sight King Jie was struck by their beauty, and he carved their names into his best jade pendant and wore it day and night. He had already tired of his queen Mei Xi, and he cast her aside like a worn-out rag.

But it is dangerous to discard a woman, and especially a queen. As she sat brooding alone in the cold and empty palace, Mei Xi's thoughts turned to her old teacher Yi Yin, who had gone back to the State of Yin. She planned a way to make use of this relationship and surreptitiously sent some officials to him with secret information about Jie's state affairs. Now when Yi Yin had returned, Prince Tang finally recognized his abilities and promoted him to the post of prime minister. Yi Yin was outraged by the excesses of Jie's court and wished to help overthrow him. The unexpected gift of information from his old queen was a gift of power, and immediately he sent men with valuable presents to quietly console Mei Xi. From that time the two remained in regular contact.

As the autumn rice bent heavy with grain awaiting harvest, Jie grew wilder. His fantastic orgies lasted for days and nights. So many officials participated that no one remained to run the state. The peasants dreaded famine that winter and feared that King Jie would snatch them from their homes and kill them for his sport. The time was ripe for Prince Tang to lead his armies against Jie.

Tang sat high on his cart driven by the official Fei Chang, who had also left Jie's court. Yi Yin sat behind him, offering counsel from his secret communications with the queen, Mei Xi.

Jie panicked and sent out his poor army; the three dukes who met Tang were trampled like ants. Their armies scattered, and Jie could do nothing but offer futile sacrifices to the Supreme God. After a few short skirmishes Jie's chief general, Xia Geng, was killed and the troops driven back. The general had been guarding the crossing of the Zhangshan Mountains, a spear in his right hand, a shield in his left. But his powerful appearance never daunted Tang, who perceived this man's dissipated nature and slashed his head off with a single swipe of his hatchet. The general reached up to find his head gone and ran away to Wushan Mountain.

Just as his army was approaching the capital, Tang had a vision. A god appeared to him saying, "I am sent by the Supreme God. I am commanded to assist you. There is now turmoil inside the capital, and when you see a fire in the northwest corner, at that time may you enter with success."

Tang pondered these words and the image of the god who had a human face and an animal's body. It had to be Zhu Rong, god of fire . . . and as he sat thinking about these things, two of his scouts burst into the tent: "Your Majesty, fire in the northwest corner of the capital!"

Indeed, Tang followed them out and saw the flames licking the sky. Tang commanded the attack, sending Jie's own surrendered troops into the battle. They stormed the northwest corner, bursting like demons out of the flames, and the impregnable palace was cast open to the eyes of the world.

Jie himself had fled with his favourite wives and Mei Xi. The courtly refugees flew in panic to a place calld Mingtiao, several hundred *li* from the capital. But Tang allowed no escape. With seventy chariots and six thousand men he pursued them as far as Mingtiao, only to discover that the clever king had gathered his remaining court officials and attendants into some broken-down ships to row southward on a river to Nanchao. They hid on a nearby lake, but the king, accustomed to his debauched and luxurious life, grew melancholy and soon died. Without a moment's remorse for his wasted life he rasped bitterly from his deathbed, "I regret nothing but one flaw of judgement, and that was in allowing the accursed Tang out of the jail at Zhongquan. Had I killed him then he would never have laid me on this straw mat today."

And with these words the king, whose senses had been sated

all during his life, let his eyelids drop and fell into the final
darkness.

King Tang Offers a Rain Sacrifice

Not long after the defeat of Xia, a terrible seven-year drought
afflicted all the lands in King Tang's domain. Streams and river-
beds ran dry, winds blew dust over the yellowed fields. The people
suffered and prayed only to hear from the official historian the
fearful prediction: We will have no rain until a human sacrifice
is made.

Tang solemnly answered with these words: "To pray for rain
is to save the people. If a sacrifice must be made, then let that
person be me."

On the day of the great rain prayer, the king walked humbly
from the palace wearing only a coarse cloak, his hair wild and
uncombed. He tied a bundle of dry grass on his back and seated
himself in a white cart pulled by a white horse. It was a strange,
subdued procession that walked to the Yin nation's most sacred
place at Sanglin. Thirsty people walked before the king, holding
up three-legged vessels and flags, blowing on flutes and beating
drums and listening to the unearthly sound of witches chanting
and wailing.

When the procession arrived at Sanglin, thousands were
standing waiting. A great pile of dry kindling had been prepared
before the altar, on which lay a sacrificial bowl containing a
single flickering flame. Groups of witches danced and made
magic around the altar.

With slow dignity, his face an expressionless mask, King Tang
rose and stepped down from his cart. He walked past the bonfire
and knelt before the altar flame, praying, "If it is I, great god, the
guilty one, let not all these innocents suffer. And if in their
ignorance these people have offended, take me, their king. For in
their stead I stand in times of prosperity, and in their stead now
I wish to stand as retribution."

On and on he prayed. A witch approached him, hacking off
his hair, cutting his nails and throwing them into the flames.
Then a witch at each elbow raised him up and led him to the top

of the woodpile. Tang stood quietly, eyes lowered, waiting for the witches to set the dry twigs ablaze.

For the timeless moment between life and death, the earth stopped turning round that terrible blazing sun. Not a person in all those thousands breathed, and suddenly the sharp crack of the witch horn filled the air. Drums beat and witches wailed, dancing around the woodpile, throwing faggots of fire from side to side until the whole dry pile was ablaze and the flames crackled up towards the king. In the fury of the flame all those people for a long hysterical moment forgot why they were there and leaned closer into the dry, thirsting heat to see their king burn.

And then came the cloud.

At first no one saw it; a strange northeast wind, a dark cloud scudding across the sky. It hung over the fire and then great round clear drops of water fell upon the land; thunder and lightning filled the sky. The king's face, eyes running and burning in the smoky flames, softened in wonder. Like a child's, his face was all open, his lips apart, his eyes wide. He turned his face to the sky and cold drops of rain rolled down his cheeks, shocking, wet. He turned his face upward to that black cloud, and tasting the sweet rain and the salt of his own tears, he felt the infinite goodness of being alive.

And so those people were saved from their seven-year drought; and so those people praised their king.

The Official Fu Yue Becomes a Star

More than a dozen generations after King Tang, a wise king called Wu Ding ascended the throne. The state had passed its zenith and was beginning again to decline, but the young prince Wu Ding showed a great passion for state affairs and the welfare of the people. When he was made king, he pledged to revive the State of Yin, to give it the strength and prosperity it had known in its youth. He lacked only one thing, he felt, and that was a wise official to assist him.

He laboured long over this problem, and for three years after the death of his father he mourned by keeping complete silence.

Even when his words were required by his officials, he only wrote them on scraps of paper.

One night as he lay sleeping he had a dream in which he met a hunchbacked labourer clad in a garment of rough gunny. The man was working beside a stream with a stake and had a piece of string over his shoulder. In the dream Wu Ding walked towards him and discovered that he was a prisoner helping to build a road. The prisoner looked up and his face was not coarse, but had a surprising aura of wisdom. Wu Ding thought the face familiar but could not place it. The prisoner and the king talked together of state affairs, and every word was powerful and touched deeply Wu Ding's heart. He was just going to ask the prisoner his name . . . when he woke up.

Wu Ding rose immediately and carved the image of the hunchback on a piece of hardwood to give to his officials. Then he wrote a speech describing the wise man of his dream, asking the people to search for him. This picture and speech were carried to all corners of the kingdom.

After much long searching some of Wu Ding's officials discovered a prisoner in a place called Fuyan near the North Sea. They observed him carefully. He wore a gunny garment. He had a piece of string over his shoulder. He was repairing a road damaged by spring torrents from the mountain. He was a little hunchbacked, and his face resembled the man in the picture. His name was Yue.

To find this old prisoner who so resembled the king's sketch was like finding an impossible treasure. They entreated him to return with them to the king, and they carried him back in their cart.

The moment Wu Ding saw the old prisoner he knew his dream had been true. He was amazed and overjoyed, for finally this was the man he sought as his adviser. All the court waited, and in awe heard the first word uttered by Wu Ding in three years:

"Welcome."

With quiet dignity the man approached the king. Together they sat and talked, the man with the confidence of a practised scholar. Together they sat and talked, together they knew the harmony of those who understand.

So Wu Ding told him all about his long silent waiting and his dream. He asked the man to become prime minister of the State of Yin. Because he had been found in a place called Fuyuan, the people called him Fu Yue.

Fu Yue was a worthy prime minister. He embraced his state duties with vigour and for the rest of his life worked harmoniously side by side with the king. At their first meeting he had given the king back his power to speak.

This Fu Yue had lived serendipitously, rising from prisoner to prime minister all because of a dream. And people say that when he died, his spirit rose into the sky to become a little glittering star of the east between Scorpio and Sagittarius. After him, this star was named "Fu Yue".

Zhou, Last King of the Shang Dynasty

Certain patterns repeat in the rise and fall of dynasties, and in this story we have a classic example. Just as Jie was a tyrant and the last king of the Xia Dynasty, Zhou was a tyrant and the last king of the Shang Dynasty. Their debauches and the stories of excess, women and wise officials who suffer are all similar. Interestingly, both tyrants jail their greatest rivals only to release them later, and this single act of mercy is what finally destroys them.

Zhou was a handsome man, skilled and strong. Bare-handed, he could fight fierce beasts of prey; alone he could pull a cart usually drawn by two strong oxen. Zhou was also witty and eloquent; none could match his powers of persuasion. But he misused his talents. He let fly his wit only to mask his own mistakes and in defiance of the people who criticized him; he only pleased himself, despising even his closest officials. Proud and self-satisfied, he called himself by the title King of Heaven.

Now this "king of heaven" never hesitated to exploit his people if there was a chance of sating his desires. For seven years he forced his subjects to build a great tower called Lutai, which was a mile wide and over a thousand feet tall. Each pavilion on the tower reached closer to the heavens until at the top the king could feel he had risen above the clouds themselves.

Zhou also liked to collect fine horses, highly bred dogs, rare birds and beautiful women from throughout the kingdom. He forced the people to offer these gifts to him at his palace. Within the city walls, the capital called Zhaoge, he built many gardens and towers to house these tributes. It is said that he had pools filled with wine and meat hung in the trees. He would order men and women to run naked after each other, carousing through the meat woods and wine pools. His music officials were asked to compose lewd music with lewd dances, and so the people, glutted with wine and food and love, remained entwined and idle day after day.

Zhou did not fear public opinion but kept it tightly under control. Anyone who dared to breathe a word against him was punished on an instrument called the *paoge*. Copper bars soaked in oil were heated over a fire and the prisoner was then placed barefoot upon it and forced to walk on the burning, slippery bars. If he slid and fell, a fire below burnt him to death. Zhou and his favourite officials would amuse themselves while observing this torture, joking about grace and cooked meat.

It is said that Zhou's cook once made bear's paw for the king, but that it was not well prepared. In a rage Zhou cut off his head. Another time he stood at the top of Lutai tower early in the morning watching an old man on the bank of the Qishui River, testing the water. The king asked his servants why he did so, and they replied, "The marrow of an old man is not solid, so he fears the morning cold. Perhaps that is why he tests and hesitates."

At once Zhou's morbid curiosity was roused. He ordered his guards to bring the man to him. Without a word they dragged him quaking before the king, cut off his foot, and held up the bloody appendage to Zhou so he could see if the marrow was solid.

Zhou had an uncle called Bi Gan who was honest and straightforward in character. Gently he tried to persuade his nephew towards greater moderation, but Zhou, tired of the advice, finally spat out: "I am told that the heart of a wise man has seven holes. I wonder if it is true."

With that he ordered Bi Gan's heart torn out and held before his dying eyes to look for holes.

When Zhou heard that a man named Jiu Hou had a beautiful and virtuous daughter, he ordered her sent to the palace to serve as a concubine. But the gentle girl refused. Thereupon Zhou

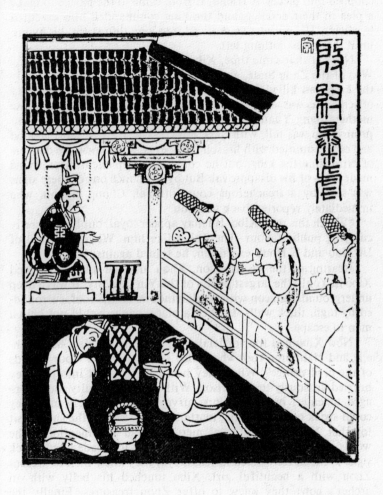

sentenced both her and her father to death and the father's body chopped into pieces. A friend, E Hou, came to the palace to make a plea in their defence, and the king commanded him executed by slicing. His muscles were sliced into long thin strips, bit by bit, until there was nothing left.

Now, at that same time, Xibo Chang, who later became King Wen of the Zhou State, grew angry when he heard how lawlessly the king had killed Jiu Hou and E Hou. Xibo was no ordinary official. He was a descendant of the foundling Hou Ji, whose mother, Jiang Yuan, had given birth after stepping into a footprint. Xibo was tall, with dark brown skin. He was short-sighted and often squinted with his scholarly eyes. Xibo knew the dangers of criticizing the king, but he could not keep silent. Secretly he made signs of his disapproval. But by ill chance one of these signs was seen by a treacherous court official, Chong Houhu, who immediately reported back to Zhou.

"Watch this man Xibo. He may appear loyal, but he is secretly currying public favour. The dukes like him. When he heard of Jiu Hou and E Hou's execution, he signed against you."

Hearing of the insurrection, Zhou arrested and imprisoned Xibo in Youli, the largest prison of the Yin Dynasty. It was a deep underground dungeon with small windows on the roof, surrounded by high, thick walls. In such a place, wings would not help a man to escape.

Now Xibo had four officials, Tai Dian, Hong Yao, San Yisheng and Nan Gongkuo, who called themselves the "four friends of the civil prince". When they heard he was cast into jail they hurried anxiously to the prison. With much difficulty they managed to enter, but the jailors surveyed them closely and they could speak only of trifling matters. By the end of the short visit together Xibo and his loyal men still had not mentioned the words in their hearts, but the wise Prince Xibo made a few quick signs to them. He winked his right eye; they knew then to present Zhou with a beautiful girl. Xibo touched his belly with an archer's bow; they knew to offer Zhou treasures. Finally the prince tapped his feet on the ground. They knew to make haste or Xibo's life would be in danger. Those four close officials, understanding all these signs, hurried back to make their preparations.

In those early times the kings made a habit of keeping certain hostages to control rebellions by dukes and princes. Bo Yikao, the eldest son of Xibo, was such a hostage and served as Zhou's cart driver. When his father was imprisoned, the lad was cast alive into a cauldron of boiling water and cooked into a soup. A bowl of the steaming liquid was then carried to the prison for Xibo to drink. The king amused his officials saying: "A wise man would certainly not drink the soup of his own son."

But the messengers came back and reported that the father, Xibo, had drunk it.

Zhou laughed and called out, "Who says Xibo is a wise man? He has drunk the soup of his son!"

And from that time he considered the prince to be foolish and paid him no more attention.

Meanwhile the four friends of the prince searched the kingdom for treasures. They found a beautiful girl in the State of Youshen. From the State of Quanrong they bought a wonderful horse with a colourful striped coat, fiery mane, golden eyes and a tail like the feathers of a rooster. Whoever rode the horse would live a thousand years. They had found a rare wild animal called the zhouyu, which resembled a striped tiger but had a tail three times as long as its body. It could run a thousand *li* in a single day. They found other rare birds and animals, black jade, great shells and exotic animal skins. They bribed a favourite official, Fei Zhong, and asked him to intercede for the prince. Then they ceremoniously laid out before the cruel leader all they had brought.

From his throne the greedy king looked over these treasures with delight; then his eyes fell upon the girl. Trembling and weeping a little, her young face fresh as dew, the girl was of unsurpassed beauty. The king grinned slowly and crooned, "This little treasure herself is perhaps enough to warrant the release of Xibo. . ."

And so it was that Xibo was released from the Youli jail. But it is dangerous to release a dragon to the sea or a tiger to the mountains. The freedom of good Xibo would hasten the downfall of the evil King Zhou and the inevitable destruction of the Shang Dynasty.

The Zhou Dynasty

Xibo Finds a Wise Counsellor

When Xibo was finally released from prison, he learned with horror of the death of his son and how he had drunk the soup made of his own flesh. His four officials hurried him away.

But about ten *li* from the place Xibo began to feel uneasy and started to retch. He slid down from his horse, and putting a finger in his throat he vomited up a piece of muscle that seemed to writhe on the ground as if a living thing. When he thought of the death of his innocent child, he had opened his throat in grief, and people buried the thing and called the grave "Tomb of the Vomited Son".

Upon his return to the State of Zhou, Xibo began to build up strong alliances with other princes and dukes. He was haunted by the injustice rendered him and his family and sought his chance for revenge. Although his four loyal supporters served him well, he now looked for a wise man, well versed in letters and martial arts to further assist him. He often dreamed that such a man was smiling and waving to him.

One night he had a special dream. A god clad in a black garment was standing on a ferry at Linghujin. Beside him stood an old man with a white beard and white eyebrows. The god gravely addressed Xibo Chang by name, "Chang, I bestow upon you a good teacher and loyal assistant. His name is Wang."

So first Xibo knelt and then the old man knelt too—and suddenly Xibo awoke.

As he lay thinking of the dream, Xibo reflected that he had heard talk of a wise man living in his state. But he knew nothing of him, not his home or his name or his occupation, so he called his assistants to search in every part of the region for this man he sorely needed. One day, just before going hunting, he asked a court historian to predict his future. Soon the official came back and chanted:

Go now hunt on the Weishui River,
A treasure will you find there,
Not a chi nor a dragon,

Not a tiger nor a bear,
But a wise duke, a loyal man,
An official lent by the gods.

The prince smiled for the first time in many months. He asked the historian which direction they should follow; then he gathered his men and went to Panxi on the Weishui River. There, in a deep forest, was a dark green pool. As they passed into a clearing beside a small pond, the prince was astonished to see an old man with a silvery white beard sitting in a clump of cogon grass wearing a bamboo hat and green clothes. He sat motionless holding his fishing line and did not even twitch at the snorting of the imperial horses and the clatter of carts and men.

Prince Xibo knitted his brows, scrutinizing the man from his cart. As he stared, the vision from his dream appeared to him. So he jumped off his cart and strode over. Respectfully he greeted him, and the old man replied without haste. Before a leaf could flutter in the breeze, the prince was saying, "Sir, my father once told me that when our nation had grown prosperous, a sage would arrive in the land. He had been looking forward to him for a long time. Are you this sage?"

Then he invited the old man to climb into his cart, and he personally drove back to the palace. The prince named the old man national adviser and gave him the title of Taigong Wang, which means "the one my father looked forward to".

This man is thought to be a real historical figure who was called by various names: Lu Shang, and Lu Wang. His ancestors are said to have helped Yu to control the flood. Commonly known as Jiang Taigong, he is famous in China for stories of his fishing.

Jiang Taigong had wanted to use his skills but never had a chance. He was so poor that his wife was said to have driven him out and ordered him to sell meat in the markets. But he sat thinking all day, forgetting his wares while they rotted in the sun. So the man grew old, his beard turning whiter and whiter. He moved to the bank of the Weishui River, where he could live a simple life in a hut. According to one account he fished by the river three days and nights and never caught a single fish. Hot with anger he threw his hat and clothes into the trees. But then a peasant came by and showed him how to wait calmly so as not to

frighten the fish. He tried it and caught a carp. In another carp he found a slip of cloth on which was written, "Lu Wang will be promoted in Qi."

Another account tells how he sat dangling his line in the water without bait for fifty-six years. All that time he didn't catch a thing, and then suddenly a great carp with a gold seal in its belly took his line.

In China these stories are fables about patience. If you wait long enough, opportunities will come. More subtle military and political minds have used the tales to illustrate the principle of waiting until the time is ripe. And indeed Jiang Taigong in all his years of service to different kings was famous for his sense of timing.

Some tell a different version of his story in which, when he heard that the prince was in jail, he suggested sending beautiful women and great treasures to secure his release. After this he was promoted to an important position.

After Prince Xibo found Taigong, some say he was first placed as a low-ranking official in a local area called Guantan. Within a year the place was so orderly that even the wind obeyed him and no breeze dared to blow strong enough to rustle leaves in the trees. One night Prince Xibo had a dream. In this dream he met a young woman who was weeping. She said: "I am the daughter of the god of Mount Taishan and the wife of the god of the East Sea. I wish to return to my father, but everywhere I go, strong winds and heavy rains follow me and moreover the local official at Guantan wouldn't let me through. I will tarnish his fame if I go there, but I must return to the east."

Xibo awoke and immediately sent for Taigong to interpret this dream; but before Taigong found words to answer, a messenger ran in with a report: Strong winds and heavy rains had passed into the Guantan area. Prince Xibo, who had now become King Wen, looked at his lowly official with new respect and immediately promoted him to serve as the national adviser.

No sooner was Jiang Taigong appointed national adviser than he began to use his skills in state affairs. The Zhou Dynasty grew and flourished. It annexed neighbouring states, and the capital was moved from Qixia to Feng, thus rivalling day by day the power of Shang.

The Shang king only yawned fatuously when he was told of the encroaching state. He said, "Am I not made king by the gods?" And he turned away to fondle the slipper of his nearest concubine and paid no attention to the approaching threat.

Young Prince Wu Brings Down the Shang Dynasty

Not long after the capital was moved, Prince Xibo or King Wen of Zhou died. His son Fa, given the title King Wu of Zhou, succeeded him, and the trusted Jiang Taigong remained as the national adviser.

Now King Wu, like his father, was short-sighted, and he had double rows of teeth, which were a sign of unyielding character. Soon after he came to the throne, he wanted to send his troops to punish the evil King Zhou of Shang; he asked his official historian for a sign. The prediction—an ill-omen—was read aloud, and all the civil and military officials hesitated. Then wise Jiang Taigong stepped out of the crowd. He rolled back his sleeves, and from the altar he took the turtle shell and the alpine yarrow used for making omens and smashed them on the ground. He stamped on them and loudly reproached those fighting men: "How can a dried up shell and old grass tell the future? Dispatch, go forth! Cease letting such child's play hinder the actions of men."

The king was most inspired by his spirit and dispatched the troops. The old Prince Xibo had not been long in the grave, and young Wu asked the men to disguise him as he sat on the chariot. He wanted his troops to march in the name of Prince Xibo, to further his honour and call upon his old loyalties. Sure enough, all the princes and dukes answered the summons with the exception of Bo Yi and Shu Qi, two sons of Gu Zhujun, who were hostile to the young king.

The two brothers were old men who had no more desire to rule. They had offered each other their power but finally agreed to go together to Prince Xibo to seek shelter in their old age. Just as they arrived in the capital their beloved leader died, and now the young prince wanted to march against a foreign state before his father was fully mourned. Those two old gentlemen did not approve, and on the day the troops were dispatched they stood in the way and said: "The young prince is an undutiful son."

The bodyguards were infuriated and wanted to beat them, but Jiang Taigong intervened, saying: "Never mind, leave these virtuous men be," and he ordered them dragged from the path.

So it was that King Wu's troops turned their horses eastward, breaking through every line of enemy resistance. Before long they reached Luoyi (now west Luoyang City, Henan Province), not far from King Zhou's capital, Zhaoge.

Just as they were ready to cross the Mengjin River, there was a great snowstorm. The troops could not move forward and so they made camp there, enduring driving rains and snows for more than ten days.

One morning five carts appeared mysteriously outside the camp. In each cart sat a gentleman flanked by two cavalrymen on tall grey steeds. They asked to meet King Wu. And thinking they were but envoys from dukes in distant states, the young ruler did not wish to receive them.

But the adviser Jiang Taigong looked out the door and said, "King Wu, the snow is a *zhang* thick, yet those carts have left no trails—I think we should receive them for they are no doubt immortals."

The prince saw this to be true, but he could not tell who the gods were nor where they came from. He did not wish to offend them by addressing them incorrectly. Jiang Taigong, however, had an idea.

He asked an attendant to serve a bowl of hot porridge to the guests. As the servant offered the bowl he said: "Our Excellency is unfortunately detained with a most urgent matter and cannot come to you. It is cold outside and he asks me to bring you this bowl of hot porridge to keep you warm. But to show my respect, to whom must I pass it first?"

One of the cavalrymen stepped forward politely and introduced his company: "First take it to the Lord of the North Sea, then the Lord of the East Sea, then the Lord of the West Sea, then the Lord of the South Sea and the God of Rivers He Bo. We are last, Master of Wind and Master of Rain."

After the attendant had accomplished this task, he reported back to Jiang Taigong. And Jiang Taigong advised King Wu,

"Now we are ready to receive them. There are five carts and two cavalrymen. They are the gods of the four seas and the river god He Bo with the Master of Wind and Master of Rain. The god of the South Sea is Zhu Rong. The god of the East Sea is Gou Mang. The god of the North Sea is Yuan Ming, and Ru Shou is god of the West Sea. He Bo is also called Feng Yi. The Master of Wind is called Yong and the Master of Rain, Yi. You may ask the gate official now to invite them in by their names, one by one."

Those immortals were surprised and honoured to be announced by name. They looked at one another winking and silently praised the wise prince. Then they knelt to him and once he had returned their greeting he said: "You have made a great journey in such bad weather. Will you now favour me with your counsel?"

"The Supreme God has chosen to favour the State of Zhou and to destroy the State of Yin. So we accompany the gods of wind and rain and encourage them to use their skills to help you in this war."

King Wu and Jiang Taigong were very pleased, and they settled into the camp awaiting further indications. Finally, on a clear, calm full-moon night, the weather fine, King Wu led his army across the Mengjin River. Eight hundred dukes and their troops sat singing victory songs as their ships floated on the water. At midstream a swarm of bees like *dan* birds buzzed at the helm of King Wu's ship. Their goldness shimmered against the black moonlit waters, and the king immediately ordered a picture of them drawn on his army flag. Later he named this ship "bees ship" in remembrance of that scene. And in high spirits the men disembarked from the ships and set up camp in Muye, thirty *li* from the capital of Zhaoge.

King Zhou of Shang heard that the army of King Wu had come. He put on his battle regalia for the first time in many years. It stretched snug across his belly, and his weapons were heavy in those soft hands accustomed to women and wine. He led his soldiers out to face their enemy. Knives and spears flashed in the cold winter sunlight. Eagles and vultures swooped and circled above.

The bravest of Wu's troops were the soldiers from Bashu. They led the charge, huge violent grins contorting their faces, dancing to the battle drums and flutes across the field in a grotesque parody of victory before the battle. When those slaves of King Zhou saw this army, they fell back in fear. Why fight for their despised ruler? Why die for this man who made their lives a misery on earth? Time stopped as they stared at the brave King Wu brandishing a golden axe in his left hand, a bamboo standard with its white ox tail in his left, leading thousands of men forward. As of one mind the slave soldiers scattered, and some even turned their spears on the hated tyrant. And the Master of Wind and Master of Rain swept down and mixed into the bloody fight.

King Zhou, standing well to the back of his troops, saw all was lost. He turned on his heel and fled—fled back to his dream tower, Lutai. And if the man loved extravagant display in life, so he loved it in death. He put on a cloak of pearls and jade especially prepared, and then he set himself on fire.

As the fire climbed up the gown, hotter and hotter, all those pearls and jade stones burnt to ashes except five priceless pieces of jade. These prevented the king's body from being reduced to ashes. So it was that King Wu's troops scrambled up the tower to find the dead body of the tyrant. Wu flashed his golden axe into the sky and cut off the king's head. He pierced that bloody head through with his bamboo standard and waved it with a white flag from the top of the tower for all to see that the tyranny of the reign of King Zhou of Shang had finally come to an end.

The Death of a Concubine and the Loyalty of Two Old Men

One of King Zhou's favourite concubines was the daughter of a duke called You Sushi. She had been captured and taken as a slave at an early age, and the tyrant King Zhou had been attracted by her beauty and wit. To court her, Zhou gave her fine food and gifts; quickly she picked her way towards the middle of the labyrinth of court power and was hated by many.

In some accounts her head was said to have been taken and displayed beside King Zhou's on the tower. Others say that she and another concubine hanged themselves in a secluded garden when they saw the king's head.

The passage of power is not smooth, for to lend loyalties to a new leader means betrayal of the old. In the kingdom of Zhou the two old men Bo Yi and Shu Qi believed King Wu wrong in rising against King Zhou. They were ashamed and fled to Shou-yang Mountain, where they composed songs of loyalty and lived on a wild plant called *wei*. But one day an old woman came to them and said: "I am told that you are wise men and from loyalty to the old prince will not eat the food of King Wu of Zhou. But even these wild plants belong to the Zhou Dynasty, so why do you eat them?"

So the old men's pride was wounded and they died of hunger.

Another version recounts a similar story. It is said that after a scholar called Wang Mozi came and asked them why they still ate Zhou food, they sat starving for many days. But a god was moved by their aspirations, took pity and sent them a white doe to give them milk. For several days they knelt, drinking her milk, when in their hunger they suddenly noticed how fat and delicious she looked. But the divine deer heard their idea and never appeared again, leaving those loyal old men to starve to death.

King Mu Meets a Magician and the Fairy of the West

With King Zhou dead, Prince Wu became King Wu, the founder of the Zhou Dynasty. But in four short generations the dynasty would again crumble under the leadership of King Zhao.

They say that one's greatest passion is also one's greatest weakness; this was the case of Zhao, who loved to travel. Once he was voyaging in the south and wanted to cross the Hanshui River. But the people of Chu State despised their carefree king, and so they schemed against him. They built a heavy clay boat, not with wood, but with glue, for the crossing, and when the king's group reached midstream, the glue boat, which had been soaked by the water, began to fall into pieces. They all sank to the bottom and drowned.

It was Mu, son of Zhao, who took the throne. He too loved to wander, and travelled even more than his father. The dust of his horses and carts covered the whole world.

At that time there was a magician called Hua Ren from a state far away in the west. Hua Ren had great powers. He could jump into the fire without singeing a hair on his body. He could stand in mid-air. He could walk through walls and move a city from east to west. King Mu thought he was an immortal and entertained him with great respect.

One early evening Mu held a banquet in honour of Hua Ren. The magician stood up and invited Mu to visit his state; he held out his hand and told Mu to grasp his sleeve. Together they rose to the middle of the sky. Then Hua Ren led the way into a magnificent palace covered with pearls and jade such as Mu had never seen before. After entertaining him with unknown delicacies, Hua Ren asked Mu to travel elsewhere. They arrived in a place of light shadows and wonderful colours. There was nothing but light and a strange and lovely music. But King Mu dared not stay too long. He asked Hua Ren to take him home, and the magician leaned over and gave him a violent push. The heavy mortal fell through the air and, with a start as if awakening from that moment in which sleep is neither deep nor light, opened his eyes to find himself sitting again at his own table, the supper dishes still warm.

Amazed, he asked the attendants what had happened.

"Nothing, my lord," They replied, "You nodded off for a moment."

But Hua Ren, the magician sitting by his side, winked and said: "Your body stayed here, that's true. I just took your spirit with me."

This excursion stirred Mu's yearning to see more of the world, and soon he abandoned state affairs completely and climbed into his eight-horse cart.

Now these eight horses were of strange origin. The driver Zao Fu had found them wild in the Kuafu Mountains. In fact they were the offspring of the war-horses let loose when King Wu overthrew King Zhou of Shang. The cart driver was a skilled horseman, and he caught and broke in these eight high-spirited beasts. They were called Hua Liu, Lu Er, Chi Ji, Bai Xi, Qu

Huang, Yu Lun, Dao Li and Shan Zi. They galloped swift and free as birds, covering ten thousand *li* in a single day. Their manes streamed like fire in the wind, their hoofs barely touched the ground; some even said these proud beasts had wings.

So Zao Fu offered these eight wondrous horses to King Mu and told his men to pasture them in Longchuan, the Dragon Valley on Donghai Island in the East Sea. A tall crop called *longchu*, or dragon's grass, grew there, which made even ordinary horses swift and strong.

Zao Fu had learned the skill of driving the cart from his wise teacher Tai Dou. First Tai Dou set up a pattern of wooden sticks, each one foot from the next. In three short days Zao Fu had learned to walk, then run, through the sticks without touching them. Then he was ready to learn the art of driving a cart. When his teacher had passed on all his knowledge, Zao Fu was very skilled and was appointed imperial driver.

King Mu chose an auspicious day to set out, with attending officials, on his journey. Zao Fu reined in the eight horses, who stamped and pranced, tossing their fine heads. They sprang forward, tracing a course from north to west. During this famous voyage the travellers met the river god He Bo at Yangyu Mountain and visited the Yellow Emperor's palace at Mount Kunlun. The people of Chiwu State offered King Mu beautiful girls, and the long-armed people at Heishui entertained him. Then the eight-horse cart carried him to the end of the west. They flew to Yanzi Mountain, where the setting sun hid each day. And it was there that he paused. For it was there that he met the lovely goddess Xi Wang Mu.*

King Mu approached her ceremoniously holding the beautiful white jade *gui* and the round *bi*.** His attendants followed with

---

*Though the name Xi Wang Mu literally means Queen Mother of the West, she is often presented as a god, rather than a goddess. In the *Book of Mountains and Seas*, Xi Wang Mu is depicted with a fearsome tiger's fangs and a leopard's tail, a strange god with wild hair held down under a hat. In the story of Chang E, Xi Wang Mu is a god who holds the elixir of immortality. But in this tale the god has become a beautiful goddess.

**The *gui* is a piece of long and pointed jade tablet held in the hands of ancient rulers on ceremonial occasions. The *bi* is a round and flat piece of jade with a hole in its centre, also displayed for ceremonial purposes.

bolts of fine coloured silks. Next day he held a magnificent banquet for her. Both monarchs loved music and poetry. There was much singing that night, and they honoured each other with poems.

After the banquet King Mu mounted his cart and drove to the top of Yanzi Mountain, where he instructed his men to erect a tablet on which he had carved five characters: Mountain of Xi Wang Mu. He also planted a locust tree in commemoration of their meeting.

And at their reluctant parting, the goddess Xi Wang Mu gave the king this poem:

I live in the western wilderness.
Leopards and tigers are my companions,
Crows and magpies my clowns.
Briefly you honour me.

I live in the western wilderness,
For I am the god's daughter.
Pitiful my state, my people,
I cannot follow you.

Musicians blow reed and pipe,
Players' hearts beat the music's time
For you the king of all people.
You are the gods' promise.

A Skilful Craftsman

While King Mu was on his way home from Yanzi Mountain, some people sent him a very skilful craftsman called Yan Shi. Yan Shi was granted an audience and the king said, "What are your skills?"

The craftsman answered, "I can create anything you like."

The king invited him to come back next day with his best invention. The craftsman duly returned leading a silent man clad in strange clothes. He told the king that the man could sing and dance if it would please him. The king was curious, and drawing his favourite concubine Sheng Ji and other palace maids to his side, watched the entertainment.

The strange man sang and moved his slim limbs gracefully, shaking his head. So much was he like a real man that the king forgot his entire court and leaned forward with fascination. With the final strains of the song the strange man danced very close to the concubine and briefly held her gaze. This caused the king to stand up in anger, and he ordered the craftsman beheaded.

Yan Shi was terrified. Swiftly he evaded the officials and twisted off the head of the dancer. Then he pulled off his limbs and opened his bosom. All was made of leather and wood painted in bright colours. King Mu was amazed as the craftsman pointed out the internal organs of the artificial man. When the heart was removed, the man could not sing; without his liver he could tell no direction; without his kidney his legs were still. After examining the invention carefully, the king said: "Your skills match the art of nature itself. Indeed, great work!"

And with that the craftsman, much relieved, was given an imperial cart and taken along with the king on the way back to Zhou.

The Rebellion of Prince Yan of Xu

Some princes have great aspirations and fine leadership skills but lack the will and daring to realize their dreams. They are led away from their true talents by circumstance and chance, and fall into foolishness and failure. Yan was such a man.

It is said that in the imperial palace of the State of Xu, a maid became mysteriously pregnant. After ten months she bore a strange fleshy egg which people considered ill-omened, and they dumped it beside a pond. In that place lived a lonely old woman with her dog Hu Cang. One day the dog was drinking from the pond when it found the egg and carried it home. He warmed the egg with his body for several days, and then a child was born. The baby lay supine and so was called Yan, which means "lying on the back".

When the palace officials learned of the birth of the boy child, they sent for him, and he grew up into a strange man who could turn his eyes back into his forehead. But he was intelligent and showed great benevolence to the people and was made successor to the prince.

Now when Yan became prince of the state, he forged friendly relations with neighbouring states. The people liked him, and dukes and princes praised him. Despite his great love of exotic animals and beautiful gardens, he was attentive to state affairs. He watched Mu's state decline as the king travelled more and more, and then he had an idea. He would take advantage of the disorder and seize the capital.

Carefully he began his strategy. With the excuse that communications were poor, he first dug a tunnel from the State of Chen to the State of Cai (Now Anhui and Henan provinces). During the building of this tunnel, which would allow easy access for his armies, Prince Yan found a red bow and a quiver of red arrows. Everywhere from the Yangtze to the Huaihe rivers, this was considered an auspicious sign and princes gave their support to Prince Yan until in the end he had thirty-six states behind him. He called himself king and sent his troops against the Zhou army.

But some men are not meant to fight, and Yan had little knowledge of the art of war. When the time for battle came, he had withdrawn and was away on a fishing expedition. This extra moment was all King Mu needed. For although he was travelling far away in the west when he heard of the rebellion, he rushed back. His eight horses flew over a thousand *li* in a single day. After a few small battles Yan was quickly defeated. He muffled his war drums and lowered his banners and beat a hasty retreat.

Yan and his troops escaped to Dongshan Mountain in Wuyuan County and hid deep in the mountains there. But although his ambitious scheme had failed, thousands of people who still respected him for his benevolence followed him. He lived among them in a stone house in a cave until his death.

As for King Mu and his troops, the battle was not yet over. It is said they travelled southward and were destroyed. Those who were in high positions became apes and monkeys and cranes. Those who were in low positions turned into insects. We have no fragments of what happened to the one who loved travel, King Mu. Records report a number of fine tributes offered to him by dukes of dependent states. Xihu sent him a long jade cutting knife and a luminous cup that was never empty. This cup was large enough to hold three *sheng* of liquid and was made of delicate white jade that glowed in the dark.

The cup was placed in the courtyard for evening banquets, and when it was retrieved it would be full of sweet dew that promised health and longevity. From this cup drank King Mu, lover of travel, and he was thought to have lived a long time.

Du Bo Kills King Xuan of Zhou

After the death of King Mu, several generations went by until the throne passed to the depraved and decadent tyrant Li. Li's son, King Xuan, was wiser and at first strove to make the dynasty prosperous once again. But the blossoms of his efforts bore no fruit because his father's political system continued to poison all attempts of growth. King Xuan was enticed into several unjust acts and was thought to have died at the hands of an angry ghost.

Once there was a young duke called Heng in the State of Du. Because he acted as a court official in the palace, he was addressed by the name Du Bo. King Xuan's favourite concubine Nu Jiu fell in love with the handsome Du Bo, and she wanted to seduce him. But the honest duke resisted her, first by simply avoiding her, then by rebuking her sternly. So the enraged woman cried to the king, "That man of yours, Du Bo, is worthless—he has even dared try to seduce me!"

Now the most capable man on a raging battlefield is sometimes a vulnerable toy in affairs of the heart. The king believed his favourite concubine and sent his men to imprison Du Bo in a place called Jiao (now southern Shanxian County, Henan Province). He ordered two officials, Xue Fu and Si Gongqi, to interrogate the duke by torture.

Du Bo had a friend called Zuo Ru who was indignant at such injustice. He appeared before the king to plead for his friend. But the king answered him sharply, "It is you who are unfaithful to your lord in offering excuses for your friend."

And Zuo Ru answered, "I am told that if one's lord acts correctly and one's friend acts incorrectly, then the good official must serve his lord. But if the friend is correct and the lord incorrect, then the good official stands by the side of his friend."

At this King Xuan flew into a rage, "Revise your words or you shall die!"

Zuo Ru smiled coldly. "I am also told that a man of integrity will never wish to die muddle-headed, nor seek to live by mouthing flattering words. If I must die, then I will die, to prove the innocence of my friend Du Bo and to show the mistaken judgement of a king."

Furious though King Xuan was, there was compelling strength in the dignity of this man. So he let him go and secretly sent word to kill Du Bo. But when the loyal friend heard the truth, he grieved over the despotism of his king and hanged himself.

Du Bo had uttered a few words after the long torture before his death. The innocent man called out, "My lord will kill me for guilt that is not mine. If a man's life ends in death, then my lord can rest at ease. But if a man has life after death, I will seek him out within three years' time."

Time passed. After almost three years the memory of the dead man's words was almost gone.

Then one day King Xuan called his dukes to hunt with him in a marshy area called Putian. They set out on a grand expedition with a hundred carts and a thousand men. Colourful banners and pennants fluttered in the breeze all through the wilderness.

At midday a strange cart appeared among them. The horse was white, the cart white, and the man driving it wore red with a red hat, red bow and red arrows. A murderous expression darkened his brow. People stared at him in horror. He looked exactly like Du Bo, the man tortured to death three years before.

The frightened people scattered, but Du Bo made directly for the cart of the pale king. The king tried to take up his bow, but the ghostly cart was upon him. Before he could move, an arrow pierced his chest and he jerked up and back, then fell forward, dead.

Several dukes rushed over to him. They took the corpse home, and when they looked at it they saw in amazement how the arrow had made the king jerk so violently that he had broken his back. Such is the power of the arrow of a ghost.

Bo Qi Sings a Mournful Song

Yi Jifu was a high-ranking official during the reign of King Xuan of Zhou. With his first wife he had a son called Bo Qi, and when the first wife died, he married again and had a son called Bo Feng. The two half-brothers lived together in harmony. But their mother had ambitions for her own son, and the elder boy stood in her way.

One night she whispered in her husband's ear, "It is difficult to speak of such things, but your first son, who seems so good, deceives you. He thinks me very beautiful and has even tried to seduce me."

Yi Jifu could not believe such words and turned away saying, "Why should you slander my good son in this way?"

But the woman in a rage spat out, "Watch from behind the garden wall tomorrow if you don't believe me—let your own eyes persuade you to believe what my words cannot."

And though Yi Jifu was determined not to watch, the dangerous seed of doubt had been planted.

The next morning the woman was delighted to see her husband's face looking through a window in a high building behind the garden. She had hidden some bees in her sleeves before entering the garden, and she wandered among the flowers. As was his custom, the first son passed through the garden to enter the court where each day he paid his respects to his parents. As he was hurrying past his stepmother, she cried out, "Bees! Bees!"

She waved her wide sleeves in front of her, releasing the bees in a swarm around her head. Bo Qi saw some caught in the tangle of her clothes and ran forward to brush her sleeves. But the woman cried out again and pulled back. From the high window the father saw this scene: his first son had run across the garden and pulled his stepmother violently to him. The woman seemed to cry out and pull away.

The son was surprised when a servant hurried towards him to bring him to his father. And the son was astonished and grieved when his father, without a word, beat him ferociously and banished him from the city.

So the boy left to lead a wanderer's life, carrying only his stringed instrument, the *qin*. By the time he reached a distant river, he realized that his stepmother had deceived him and he sat down and sobbed in his innocence. Long he wandered, and when the frost fell, his clothes were already worn thin. He took lotus leaves for clothes and lived on dry pear flowers. The days grew shorter and colder. As Bo Qi wandered barefoot on the frozen riverbank, he made up a song called "Trudging in the Frost", and he sang it while plucking the *qin*:

> *Cold morning, frost under my feet,*
> *Heavens I implore you.*
> *Beaten, what fault is mine?*
> *Exiled, what offence divine?*
> *Where in all this world*
> *Shall I call home.*

So sad was the sound of this music that Bo Qi slipped into the river and drowned himself. But the song had not been heard by his ears alone. There lived in that river a fairy who was saddened at the mournful notes. Under the water she gave Bo Qi a fairy medicine so he would live, then taking him by the hand, led him to an underwater palace.

Near that river, on calm, moonlit nights, it happened that the local fishermen and sailors often heard the song. They loved the haunting melody and the mournful words, and so they sang it often.

One day, Yi Jifu followed his king to hunt in the same region. They were following the riverbank and were deeply moved by the song they heard the fishermen singing, "Trudging in the Frost". The king praised the music, but in his secret heart the official wondered if this were a song of his banished son. Later the repentant father sent men out to look for the young man and was disappointed each day when they returned home alone.

And Bo Qi below the water sorrowed too, for he missed his father and half-brother. Even his music was little solace against his solitude—eventually he lost his voice and grew weaker. Even the fairy medicine could not sustain him against his grief, and there in the depths of the river he slowly died. After his death his form changed one last time, and he turned into a small long-tailed bird that flew among the mulberry trees singing, "Jueya . . . jueya. . ."

It so happened that his father was driving a cart under these mulberry trees and heard the little bird singing. When we sorrow a long time, sometimes our minds receive strange intuitions. The man called out to the bird, "If you are my son, come here; if you are not, fly back to your home in the sky."

His words were not finished when the bird landed on his cart, and the man was overcome with joy and sorrow.

"My poor son," he cried, "You have truly suffered. Come home with me."

So together they journeyed back, and when the little bird saw the courtyard where he had been betrayed, he flew over and landed on a pole by the well, singing his song of sorrow. The stepmother came out to the courtyard and said, "Where did that bird come from—its song is so tedious!"

Yi Jifu answered her sharply, "That is my poor son Bo Qi, whom I sent to wander homeless. He has changed into a bird and now returns home with me."

When the younger brother Bo Feng heard this, he came running out of the house. "Is that you, my dear lost brother! Welcome home, how I have missed you!"

But much annoyed, the woman pushed the boy away, and taking a broom from the corner, she waved it at the bird, crying, "Drive the strange bird away! It brings ill-fortune, get it away!"

Finally Yi Jifu perceived the cruelty of his wife. He took his bow from the wall and handed it to the screaming woman, "It is useless to wave your broom," he said. "Why not just shoot the bird?"

And as the woman placed an arrow on the string and pulled back the bow, Yi Jifu took up another bow and quietly shot an arrow into the back of his wife. Wailing, Bo Feng threw himself upon his mother, and the bird on the well cried out strangely. At length Yi Jifu told his second son the whole story, and from that time the bird and the son and the father lived together.

This bird is called a shrike in English. In Chinese its name is derived from the name of the boy, Bo Qi, and the words the father said to it when he recognized it as his son: "Lao ku le ma?" ("Have you suffered?") and so the bird is called *bo lao*. These birds still call sad songs that we hear on still summer days.

The Death of King You:
Fall of the Western Zhou Dynasty

After King Xuan's death, his son King You took power. At that time an aristocratic family by the name of Yi was a controlling power in the court. They sought to undermine the king and created havoc in state affairs. The people feared their cruelty and dared not speak out. Many had no means of livelihood, and ill-omens began to appear. First the three rivers Jingshui, Weishui and Loushui, all originating from the Qishan Mountains, went dry. The Qishan Mountains (home of the Zhou people) collapsed. Oxen changed suddenly into ferocious tigers, and a flock of sheep turned into a pack of vicious wolves. The people of the Loushui River were obliged to build a tower on the south bank to protect themselves. They called it *Bilangcheng,* or "shelter from wolves". These strange occurrences were seen as omens predicting the fall of a state. In the records is the story of a woman named Bao Si, who is attributed with the fall of the Western Zhou Dynasty. She was said to have come to the palace as a poor slave to atone for the crime of another person. The king met her by chance, and she was soon his favourite concubine, but the legendary stories describe her as an enchantress.

Long, long ago just before the fall of the Xia Dynasty, a pair of dragons descended from the sky and mated in the palace; they called themselves king and queen of the Bao State. The King of Xia and his officials were frightened and didn't know what to do. They could kill the dragons, leave them alone, or try to drive them away. Nobody dared to decide, and so they asked for divinations. But the omens were always unlucky until someone finally suggested that they store the dragon's semen. This time the divination was lucky. So those people took out their most beautiful containers and placed them before the dragons, praying, begging their permission. And it worked. Before long the two dragons disappeared, leaving only a little semen on the floor. The king ordered it kept in a special box, and many years passed, through the Yin to the Zhou dynasties, and none dared open the box.

Then near the end of the reign of King Li of Zhou, one day from curiosity the king opened the case. The dragon semen fell to the floor and filled the room with a horrible smell. No matter how they cleaned, they could not get rid of it. So according to the ancient belief that evil conquers evil, King Li commanded a group of women from the palace to take off their clothes and dance and shout at the semen. The women did as they were commanded, and as soon as they began to shout, the semen rolled up into a tight ball and turned into a lizard. All the court people were frightened at this strange sight and scattered away, except a young girl child who was run over by the reptile as she was not quick enough to run away. And later, after the death of Li, in King Xuan's reign, when she was older she became pregnant and bore a little girl. People were afraid of the baby and threw her outside the palace walls.

Now only one or two years before the child was thrown away, the children of the capital were heard singing this song:

Mountain mulberry bow
and beanstalk sacks
are the cause of the ruin of Zhou.

The song became popular, known to everyone in the imperial palace. King Xuan heard the song and wondered about its meaning. He sent out his men to seek the cause of the ruin, and they happened to find a mountain couple coming into the city carrying two baskets of mulberry bows and a sack of beanstalks. They walked along crying their wares: "Mulberry bows! Beanstalk sacks!"

The soldiers hurried back to tell the king, but before they could return to arrest them, the couple had been warned and hastened away. In their panic they made a wrong turn, and as they were following the city wall in the darkness to find the right path, they heard the cry of a baby.

There she lay all alone near a crack in the wall, and looking at her in the dim moonlight, they decided to adopt the girl and take her away with them. When the child was placed in their basket, she grew calm and stopped crying. All night the couple trudged along, taking turns carrying the basket, until at dawn they found their way out of the capital city. They followed a road southwest until they reached the State of Bao. There in that place they sought shelter with an aristocrat named Bao Xu and became his slaves. The girl was brought up in the family and became a slave herself; because she had no name of her own, she was named after her master and called Bao Si.

One day the master Bao Xu went to the capital of King You and was imprisoned for a reason that was not known. But as he sat there in prison, he thought of his lovely slave girl and asked if she could come to serve in the palace in exchange for his release from the prison. This was agreed to; Bao Si entered the palace as an imperial maid. Bao Xu returned home freed from jail.

The enchanting girl had several extraordinary characteristics. For example, although she rapidly rose from slave girl to become the king's favourite concubine, enjoying all the comforts of the palace, she rarely smiled. The king tried everything to please her, but still she would not smile. Her secret grief lay locked away in her heart.

At that time, border areas were guarded with many beacon towers. When there was an emergency, fires were lit on the towers which meant that a rescue was needed. These beacons were one of the safeguards of the state. These were called *langyan*, which means "wolf's smoke", because the burning fires were fed with dried wolf dung. Such fires smoked heavily, and the smoke rose in the air as a signal.

But in the company of the enchanting concubine the king became a frivolous man. Trying to make Bao Si smile, he ordered his men to go and light a beacon fire and begin the rolling of the war drums. Immediately other beacons lit up in response, and dukes rushed from all over the nearby vassal states with their armies to the capital. When they found they had been deceived, they went back to their homes angry.

Bao Si was taken to the watch tower by the king. Seeing all those upset and angry people returning down the dusty roads, she suddenly smiled and laughed for the first time. The king was so pleased that whenever he wanted to make his concubine smile, he had the beacon fires lit.

Some time later Bao Si gave birth to a son named Bo Fu. The king was very happy and wanted to make her queen, but his first wife was Shen, sister of Duke Shen. Much earlier she had borne a son called Yi Jiu, who was considered crown prince, heir to the throne. All this stood in the way of Bao Si's promotion, and so a wicked idea came to him—he would murder his first son.

One morning the young crown prince was playing in the garden where the wild animals were kept. The king sent one of his men to release a tiger, which leapt towards the boy. Quick-witted and brave, the boy opened his eyes and roared at the tiger just as he had seen the tiger tamer do. The beast was fooled and flopped lazily to the ground.

Once foiled, the king still resolved to put Bao Si on the throne. He told his wife that he was abandoning her, and after he had made several more attempts on his first son's life, the boy finally ran away. Then Bao Si was made queen, and her son Bo Fu crown prince.

Duke Shen, the king's brother-in-law, was at that time a powerful leader with allegiances from the states of Zeng, Xi Yi, and Quan Rong. He was so angry at King You's behaviour towards his sister and at the appointment of the wicked Guo Shifu as prime minister that he called on the troops of those three states to come and attack the capital with him. King You was terrified to hear of the approaching army, and he lit the beacons to call for reinforcement troops to help him. But not a single duke came.

The king fled eastward from his palace towards Lishan Mountain with the concubine Bao Si, but before they could escape, the Quan Rong army overtook them. King You was killed, and Bao Si captured and carried west.

Other dukes supported the former crown prince as king, and he was called King Ping. By then the nation of Quan Rong was growing stronger and stronger. The new King Ping had to move his capital from Gaojing to Luoyi in the east to protect himself from Quan Rong. But from that time the Zhou Dynasty weakened until it almost disappeared, remained only in name and in memory.

Chapter 6
OTHER FAVOURITE TALES

The Foolish Old Man Removes the Mountains

Once there was an old man, ninety years old, called Yu Gong (Foolish Old Man), who lived in the Beishan Mountains. Two great peaks, Taihang and Wangwu, stood in front of his house. Each time he had to climb over those peaks, he cursed them for blocking his way. For a lifetime he had cursed those mountains.

One day he called his family together and said: "I am tired of these two mountains always in the way. All my life I've had to climb over them. Let's move them elsewhere."

His sons and grandsons all agreed: "All right!"

But his wife said: "What nonsense! An old man like you couldn't even move a small hill. How do you expect to move two great mountains? And even if you could, where would you put the earth and rocks?"

Those foolish sons and grandsons all replied, "That's easy. We'll just carry them to the shore of the Bohai Sea."

So they started to work at once. They dug into the mountain and carried the earth bucket by bucket to the Bohai Sea. Even the young child of the widow Jing Chengshi came to help them. And after half a year they had made only one trip back and forth. They left wearing their cotton padded coats and returned wearing only light shirts.

Now the wiseman of Hequ saw this, and he laughed at the foolish old man.

"I say, old man, why not stop now? You are old and ailing; your life is like the flickering flame of a candle in the breeze. What can you do against a great mountain?"

The Foolish Old Man answered, "You are wrong. Don't you know that when I die, my sons will continue my work, and when my sons die, my grandsons will continue too? And these grandsons will have sons. We will continue our work from generation to generation. Why can't these mountains be moved? You are really no smarter than the widow Jing Chengshi's young son."

And the wiseman had no answer.

It happened that a god holding a snake in his hand was listening to this conversation. He feared that if the old man really stuck with this foolishness, the two famous mountains might be overcome. He hurried to tell the Supreme God. The great god was deeply moved by the staunch spirit of the old man, however, and he sent two giant sons of Kua Eshi to help the old man remove the mountains. One of the mountains was taken to Shuodong in the east and the other to Yongnan in the south.

Sea Creatures

People have always watched the endless waves of the sea and the changing colours of the clouds over its surface. And below that mysterious surface they have seen such wonders as the underwater palace of the dragon king, oyster nymphs, turtle monsters, and serpent demons. In China there are many legends about mermaids and giant crabs.

Once there was a merchant who sailed abroad on business. After days and days of sailing, he spotted a small island covered with thick trees. The merchant was happy to see land once more, and he ordered his sailors to drop anchor.

Together they took a small boat to the island, gathered some kindling, and built a small fire to cook their lunch. Hardly was the pot of water boiling when first one, then another, looked around to see if anyone else had noticed a vague trembling in the ground. Suddenly the land lurched to one side, the trees began to sink, and all the men jumped up and ran to their skiff on the beach. Too frightened to pull up anchor, they cut the painter and hoisted the sail to hurry away. But when they turned to look back, they saw what it was. They had not built their fire on an island at all, but on a giant crab whose shell they had burnt while making their lunch.

The earliest stories of mermaids say that these strange creatures had fish bodies and human faces, with hands and feet just like a person. Their name, *ling fish*, means "fish who can live on the land", and they were the same as the famous dragon fish ridden by the witch in the story of Yi and Chang E.

Mermaids could be fierce creatures. Some people say there lived in the South China Sea a group of mermaids and mermen called *jiaoren*. These creatures spent their time weaving at shuttles, and if you stood on the beach on a calm starry night, you could hear the sound of their weaving rising out of the waters. The *jiaoren* often wept like people, but though their feelings were the same, their tears were different. They wept teardrops that turned into pearls. Both male and female *jiaoren* were very beautiful, with jadelike skin and hair as long as a horse's tail. If you gave them wine to drink, their skin would turn pink as the peach blossom and even more beautiful. In the old days people used to say that if you lost your wife or your husband, you could get a mermaid or a merman to keep in a pond and think of it as your loved one.

The Origin of the Cuckoo

In ancient times in the State of Shu the people wandered from place to place following their king, Can Cong. These people had eyes in the middle of their foreheads, and when people found their burial places later, they called them "tombs of standing-eyed people." King Can Cong taught those people how to raise silkworms, and wherever they wandered they grew prosperous with the silkworm trade.

The successor of King Can Cong was Bai Guan, and his successor was Yu Fu, who first made his capital in Qushang (now Shuangliu County, Sichuan Province) and then moved it to Pi (now Pixian County, Sichuan Province). Yu Fu later became immortal and turned into a fairy while hunting in the Jianshan Mountains.

Many years had passed after King Yu Fu left the state, when a man called Du Yu descended from the heavens to Zhuti (now Yibin County in Sichuan Province). And a woman called Li appeared out of a well near a river. These two were married and Du Yu now calling himself Wang Di, made himself king of the State of Shu, and set up the capital in Pi. He was a wise leader, teaching people farming skills—how to follow the seasons and increase their harvest. But he could do nothing about the frequent floods.

One year a strange thing happened. A corpse was floating on the river, upstream against the current. People pulled it out, and to their astonishment it stood up and said, "My name is Bie Ling (Turtle Spirit), I come from the State of Chu."

When Wang Di heard of this strange occurrence, he sent for the man. As they talked together, Wang Di saw that Bie Ling was an intelligent man who had a special knowledge of the nature of water. And so he appointed Bie Ling prime minister in the hope that he could deal with the floods.

The next flood in the land was where Yulei Mountain blocked the natural flow of the waters. Some people say that Bie Ling led the people to dig a pass through Yulei Mountain to the Minjiang River. But others say that the pass was opened through Wushan Mountain, allowing the flow of the great Yangtze.

So pleased was King Wang Di of Shu with this work that he even asked Bie Ling to succeed him as the king of their state. Bie Ling thus became the king and was given the title Kai Ming Di or Cong Di, both meaning "the enlightened king". King Wang Di retired to Xishan Mountain to live in seclusion.

Soon it was rumoured that King Wang Di had had a love affair with Bie Ling's wife. The former king was much shamed that Bie Ling might hear such stories after returning from conquering the flood, so he lived in seclusion deep in the mountains. He regretted too that he had made such a blunder as to relinquish the power of the kingdom. And so it was that he died in deep sorrow and regret.

His spirit changed into the cuckoo bird. This bird sang out gloomily.

And people say that it cries until blood flows from its mouth.

Duke Ping of Jin Hears Divine Music

During the Spring and Autumn Period (770–476 BC) there lived in the State of Jin a duke called Ping who loved music. One day while he was entertaining Duke Ling of the State of Wei and his entourage, it came to his attention that one of the men in the group was an accomplished musician called Shijuan. He was duly invited to play, and he played something called "jingshang", but the duke was not satisfied.

He asked his own musician Shi Kuang, "Is this indeed the most touching music?"

"Your Majesty, I am afraid not, 'jingzhuang' is more touching."

"Then let it be played!"

Shi Kuang took out his stringed instrument and began to play, and a wondrous thing happened. Sixteen cranes flying from the south swooped down into the hall and danced to the delight of all the guests. The duke toasted his musician with wine and asked again, "Is this indeed the most touching music?" "Your Majesty, I am afraid not, 'jingjiao' is more touching."

"Then let it be played!"

There was a silence and then Shi Kuang said, "Your Majesty, this is divine music composed by the Supreme Emperor of the Heavens himself when he gathered all the ghosts and demons at the famous procession of Xitai Mountain. It cannot be played at will . . . for if it is, disasters will befall all mortals."

Duke Ping of Jin scoffed and ordered the musician to proceed. Trembling he began, and clouds in the west began to rise up into the sky. Strong winds blew in, tearing away the curtains, smashing dishes on to the floor; hail thundered down on the palace, shattering the tiles of the roof. The guests scattered in all directions, and the duke himself hid trembling in a corner. And when the storm subsided, a drought blighted the land for three long years. This was the punishment of the god; this was the terrible power of "jingjiao", the Supreme Emperor's divine music.

The Herdsman and the Weaver Girl

The famous story of the two stars, Altair and Vega across the Milky Way, is as known and loved now throughout China, as it has been for centuries.

A long time ago when the Silver River (Milky Way) was a shallow stream and still touched the earth, there lived in the sky a fairy, a weaving girl who was the granddaughter of the Queen of Heaven. It was her job to weave colourful clouds called the "clothes of heaven" to hang in the sky, all different for the different days and seasons.

Far away on the other side of the shallow Silver River lived an orphan herder called Niu Lang. His parents had long been dead, and his elder sister and brother left him all alone with only an old ox.

The boy toiled alone in the fields. He built a wooden house and had only the silent ox as his companion.

One day that ox opened its mouth and told the young man a strange story. It told him about a weaving maid and six other fairies who often bathed in the Silver River. It told him if he stole her clothes while she was bathing, she would become his wife.

The boy went that night to the bank of the river and hid himself in the reed marsh. Sure enough, at dusk, the girl weaver and six fairies appeared. They took off their garments and plunged into the clear stream. They looked like lotus flowers floating there on the waves.

Quickly the young herdsman snatched away the girl weaver's clothes. The rustle of the reeds frightened those fairies and they flew off, leaving the girl all alone.

And so she became his wife.

For a long time they lived happily together, the herdsman toiling in the fields, the young wife weaving at home. And they had two children and thought they would live a life of love together for ever.

But it was not to be. When the Heavenly God and Queen Mother learned that the weaving maid had stayed on earth, they sent for her to punish her in the heavenly palace. So the girl was taken away from her husband and children, and the anguished young herdsman put their children in two baskets, one at each end of a carrying pole, and set out to find his wife. He hurried towards the place where he had first stolen her clothes but was astonished to see that the river was no longer there. The angry Queen Mother had taken the river back to the heavens with her divine power. The poor man turned his eyes up and peered into the blue night. There shone that bright river in the sky, keeping mortals away from immortals.

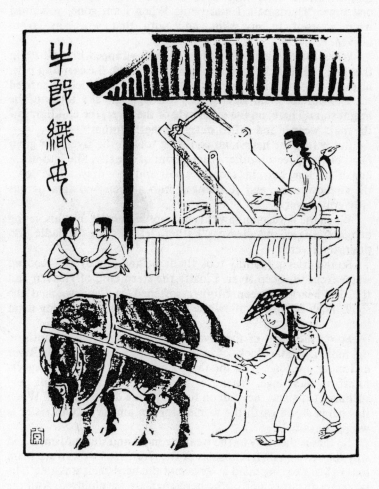

So he returned to his home with his children, and together they mourned. And then their old pet, the ox, spoke a second time: "Herdsman, I am dying. When I am gone, you must wrap yourself in my skin, and with that you can go to heaven."

When the ox died soon after, the man wrapped himself up in the skin, and then, to balance his two baskets on the carrying pole, he put a long ladle into one of the two baskets in which he carried the two children. He flew swiftly through the sky towards the bright stars. There, on the other side of the river, the children saw the maid weaver and called out, "Mother! Mother!"

But before the herdsman could set foot in the river, the great hand of the Queen Mother reached out of the sky. She had taken one of her long hairpins from her hair and now drew a line down the shallow river, and it changed into a deep and treacherous Heavenly River.

When the herdsman saw this he wept in despair. But his young daughter tugged his sleeve: "Father, let us take the ladle and drain the river."

So the grieving family took the ladle and one by one scooped water from the deep river. Finally the stern God of Heaven and the cold-hearted Queen Mother softened as they watched the sight. They decided to allow the herdsman and the weaving maid to meet once a year.

So on the night of the seventh day of the seventh month on the lunar calendar flocks of magpies soar across that Silver River and make a bridge. And the family crosses the bridge and meets to affirm their love. Whenever they meet, the wife cannot help shedding tears and they fall on the earth in a drizzling rain. When this happens, on earth the women sorrow and say: "Our sister is weeping again."

So that is the story of the weaving maid and the herdsman and why they live on different sides of the river. And we still see them today. The weaving maid is Vega and the herdsman is Altair. The two stars on either side of the herdsman are his children. And the other four bright stars beside him are said to be the shuttles of the weaving girl's loom on which she sends him messages. The three stars beside the weaving girl are her husband's messages. And thus these bright stars in the autumn sky remind us of eternal love.